Stealing Home

Stealing Home

ELLEN SCHWARTZ

Tundra Books

Text copyright © 2006 by Ellen Schwartz

Published in Canada by Tundra Books,
75 Sherbourne Street, Toronto, Ontario M5A 2P9

Published in the United States by Tundra Books of Northern New York,
P.O. Box 1030, Plattsburgh, New York 12901

Library of Congress Control Number: 2005927012

Library and Archives Canada Cataloguing in Publication

Schwartz, Ellen, 1949-
Stealing home / Ellen Schwartz.

ISBN-13: 978-0-88776-765-4
ISBN-10: 0-88776-765-6

I. Title.

PS8587.C578S84 2006   jC813'.54   C2005-902921-8

We acknowledge the financial support of the Government of Canada
through the Book Publishing Industry Development Program (BPIDP)
and that of the Government of Ontario through the Ontario Media
Development Corporation's Ontario Book Initiative. We further
acknowledge the support of the Canada Council for the Arts and the
Ontario Arts Council for our publishing program.

ONTARIO ARTS COUNCIL
CONSEIL DES ARTS DE L'ONTARIO

Design: Terri Nimmo
Typeset in Minion

Printed and bound in Canada

This book is printed on acid-free paper that is 100% recycled,
ancient-forest friendly (100% post-consumer recycled).

1   2   3   4   6   11   10   09   08   07   06

For Bill, who has a bit of Joey in him.
And for Dad, who always cries.

1

Joey Sexton tossed a baseball over his head, caught it in his glove, then transferred it to his bare hand. Threw it again, higher this time, caught it. Higher still, in a looping arc, ran to catch it. *Smack.*

"And DiMaggio makes another spectacular grab in centerfield!" he said out loud, pitching his voice nasal and tinny like Mel Allen, the Yankees' announcer. He trotted down the street, tossing the ball back and forth. Stuffing poked out from a side seam of his glove, and the strap on the back, where the stitching had come loose, flapped when he whipped his hand out, but he paid it no mind. No chance of getting a new glove now, not with Mama gone, so he might as well stop wishing.

Barely a breeze stirred the humid air, and Joey's damp shirt stuck to his back. Throwing and catching, announcing the action in a steady patter, he jogged past old apartment buildings where dark-skinned ladies sat, fanning themselves with newspapers at the top of tall stoops, and babies, dressed only in diapers, dozed on blankets at their feet.

"DiMaggio fires to first –" Joey stepped into the street, making the throw. A loud, deep horn blasted, and he looked up to see a dump truck bearing down on him.

"Watch where you're going, kid!"

"Aw, keep your shirt on," Joey yelled, but he quickly stepped back. Waiting for the light, he went into a batter's stance, cocking an imaginary bat over his shoulder. A long, slender bat of pure blond ash – *Louisville Slugger* branded on in brown letters. He pulled a tattered baseball card from his back pocket and studied the picture, then replaced the card. Shifting his weight more onto the balls of his feet to match DiMaggio's stance, he lifted his right elbow an inch higher.

"And here's Joltin' Joe himself to lead off the inning," he announced in the same nasal voice. "DiMaggio steps into the box. Takes a practice cut. Look at that powerful swing. The pitcher winds up. He delivers –" Joey swung his arms around, tight and fast, like DiMaggio, his feet swiveling but not lifting off the ground, channeling all the power of his arms and shoulders and hips. "It's a line drive! DiMaggio's safe at first. How about that!"

The light changed. Joey sprinted across the inter-section, imagining himself sliding into second for a stolen base. True, DiMaggio wasn't so hot on stolen bases. Not like that new fellow, Jackie Robinson. It was only June, and he already had ten. Fast? Shoot! He was a speed demon. But Robinson was on the Dodgers – the hated Brooklyn Dodgers.

Joey turned the corner and scanned the abandoned field at 157th Street and Courtlandt Avenue, where Harry and some of the other boys sometimes gathered for a game. Nobody there. Shucks. Well, maybe they were at the schoolyard.

Heading down a different street, he threw the ball up as high as he could. "With two outs in the top of the ninth and the Yankees leading the White Sox by a run, Luke Appling hits a high fly to center. DiMaggio's running back, back . . . He's got it to end the inning and win the game! My, what a start the Bronx Bombers have had this year! Coming off a disappointing '46 season, they're back on track to win the pennant. . . ."

Joey turned a corner. There loomed the massive red brick P.S. 82 with its double cement staircases leading to the Boys' and Girls' wooden entrance doors. Prison during the school year, complete with bars over the windows to guard against errant balls; playground in the summer. Joey dragged his glove along the chain-link fence that ran around the school. *Thwackeda, thwackeda, thwackeda.* Voices sounded from the back. Somebody had a game going – he hoped it was Harry and those fellows. Squeezing through the gap where the fence was broken, he circled around to the rear of the school.

Shoot. Jerome and his gang. The Negroes. Six or eight of them, a few boys crouching at the ready in the field – if you could call it a field. It was more like a gravel patch, the odd tuft of weeds sprouting through the pebbly dirt. The tall skinny kid, Donny, was at bat, and Jerome, as usual, was on the mound. As Joey watched, Jerome wound up. *Zoom.* Boy, that kid could pitch. He was a head taller than Joey, and twice as strong. Donny swung. Grounder to short. Maurice – a small boy who always tagged along behind Jerome like a skittish shadow – scooped it up. Donny dove for first, sending up a cloud of dust, as Maurice made the throw.

"One out!" Jerome sang.

"Darn!" Donny said, retrieving the bat – a Louisville Slugger.

Maybe this time, Joey thought. Sooner or later they'd break down. He inched forward.

"Hey, fellas."

Jerome turned, made a face. "You again. What do you want?"

"Can I play?"

"No." Jerome turned to face the next batter.

"Aw, come on," Joey said, approaching third base.

"You heard him," Donny said.

"You only got seven," Joey argued. "I'll even out the sides."

"Forget it."

Joey edged closer. "Hey, come on, I can hit."

"Yeah, but how're you going to field with that worn-out raggedy thing?" Donny said, pointing to Joey's glove. The other boys laughed, their teeth white in dark brown faces.

"Stuffin's fallin' out."

"Flap-flappety-flap," Maurice said, flapping his arms like a chicken.

Joey's cheeks burned. "So what if my glove's old? That doesn't mean –"

Jerome jerked his thumb. "Get lost, whitebread."

That name again. "Don't call me that," Joey said in a low voice.

"Aw, hurt your feelings?"

"I mean it."

Jerome grinned at the others. "We don't want no crackers in our game, do we, boys?"

"Shut up!" It wasn't the words that infuriated Joey so much as the way they were said. As if there was something

5

wrong with being half white. Or half black, for that matter. Who cared? But no one was going to rag him about it and get away with it. He dropped his glove and flung himself at the taller boy.

Surprised, Jerome stumbled back, but quickly recovered. Tossing his glove to the shortstop, he shoved Joey. Joey saw his nostrils flare, his lips press into a brown line. The other boys closed in.

"Shut him up, Jerome!"

Joey flailed with his fist, but only grazed Jerome's cheek. It was enough to enrage the other boy, however, who responded with a blow to Joey's shoulder that made him stagger.

"Attaboy, Jerome."

Regaining his balance, Joey swung upward. His fist plowed into the soft pillow of Jerome's stomach, and Joey felt keen satisfaction to see him grimace, to hear him grunt. But a moment later, Jerome landed a sharp blow to Joey's mouth. He felt a sting, tasted blood. He lashed out, but missed. Jerome laughed.

"Show him, Jerome."

Joey stepped in closer, swung, and connected with Jerome's jaw. The other boy hit him on the side of the head, knocking him to the ground. Sharp pebbles dug into his bottom, the backs of his legs. Before he could react, Jerome hauled him up by the shirt. Joey heard the fabric rip. Shoot! Mrs. Webster had already reamed him out for tearing this same shirt the other day. Furious, he jumped on Jerome, swinging wildly.

"You dirty, rotten —"

So intent was he on trying to hit Jerome that he didn't notice that the others had fallen silent, until he felt a strong grip on his arm. Thinking it was one of the boys, he tried to shake it off. "Let go —"

"What in God's name you think you're doing?"

An ebony face, framed by a straw hat with wisps of frizzy gray hair sticking out, was frowning down at him.

"Mrs. Webster!"

"Get out of there."

"But Mrs. Webster —"

"You scoundrel, I can't turn my back one minute and you're in trouble."

"They started it —"

"Don't you give me backtalk, boy."

"Let go of me," he yelled, trying to wiggle free, but her fingers dug in painfully. *For an old lady*, he thought, *she sure has a powerful grip.*

"Move — *now!*" she ordered.

At least the other boys were as much in awe of her as he was, and didn't laugh. Somehow Joey managed to scoop up his ball and glove before he was dragged around the corner into a rundown building, up four flights of stairs, and deposited in the front hallway of Mrs. Webster's apartment.

She regarded him, hands on hips. She was panting, and Joey hoped she wasn't going to have one of her "breathing spells." That was all he needed – to make Mrs. Webster faint.

Turned out she had breath enough. "What'm I gonna do with you, Joey Sexton? Minute I turn my back, you're in a fight. And now your shirt is tore again –"

"He started it. Callin' me names –"

"And if it's not fightin', it's some other grief. Last week of school you got sent to the principal's office for sassin' the teacher. And before that the cops brought you home for throwing rocks at windows." She shook her head. "Now look at you – all tore up, with a bloody lip and a swollen head. I swear, you're more trouble than you're worth."

Joey put his hands on his hips. "Then why don't you just throw me out?"

"And let you run wild in the street?" She snorted. "Not likely."

"None of your business anyway," he grumbled.

"Hush your mouth. I made a promise to your mama, and I mean to keep it!"

She stopped as Joey's eyes filled with tears. He folded his arms across his chest.

"Aw, come here, boy." She pulled him to her. "I didn't mean to make you feel bad."

Joey twisted away. "Don't need you," he said, but his voice trembled. He didn't want to think about how he'd sobbed on her shoulder after Mama died. How he'd shadowed her, afraid to leave her side, for days. Scowling, he dashed away the tears with his sleeve.

The telephone rang, and Mrs. Webster went into the kitchen to answer it. Joey dried his eyes and wiped his nose. Meddling old busybody. . . .

"Oh, hello, Miss MacNeill," Mrs. Webster said. "How're you today?"

Joey froze.

Miss MacNeill was the social worker who'd been assigned to his case after his mother died. For the past few months, while Joey stayed with Mrs. Webster in the apartment across the hall from where he and Mama had lived, Miss MacNeill had been trying to track down his father.

Joey had only vague memories of his daddy. In fact, he knew only three things about him: his name was Horace Sexton, he was colored, and he was a trumpet player. Joey's ears remembered the liquid notes of his daddy's trumpet, melting in the air. His body remembered being thrown up high and caught by warm, strong hands; being tickled by long brown fingers. He had fuzzy recollections of nights when the room was full of bodies, the smell of sweat and spicy food, dancing and laughter and loud music. And he remembered crying sometimes when no one paid any attention to him and his diaper chafed and his tummy growled.

Joey didn't remember when his daddy left, though he recalled voices shouting and people fighting. Mama had told him that his daddy had lived with them off and on for a couple of years, first in Kansas City, where Joey was born, then in Chicago, then in the Bronx. Then his daddy had gone back to Chicago to play a gig and was never heard from again.

But that didn't mean his daddy wasn't out there some-where. Or that he didn't love him. Or that, when he learned how his son needed him, he wouldn't come right away. Of course he would. Something had prevented him all these years, Joey was certain. Probably his career. He was a musician, after all. Had to travel the world – London, Paris, Rome. . . . It was no surprise that he'd lost touch. But now, Joey was just as certain that nothing would keep him away.

He edged toward the kitchen, straining to figure out from Mrs. Webster's replies what Miss MacNeill was saying.

"Yes, Miss MacNeill, ten o'clock. That'll be fine," Mrs. Webster said. "See you then." She hung up.

Heart pounding, Joey asked with his eyes.

"She has news. Wants us to come in tomorrow."

Until that moment, when he let out his breath, Joey didn't realize he'd been holding it. He whooped. "She's found him! She's found my daddy!"

"Now, Joey –"

"That must be it. What else could it be?" He grinned, barely noticing the pain of his swollen lip.

"Now, don't you go getting all excited."

Joey brushed that off with a wave of the hand. "Where do you suppose he is?" He started pacing the narrow kitchen. "D'you think he still lives in Chicago? I hear it's a swell town. They got Comiskey Park –"

"Joey."

"I bet he's rich, a real big shot. And he'll come get me in a shiny new car –"

"Stop now."

"– and we'll live in a fancy house with all the food you could ever want."

"Joey!"

"He'll buy me a new glove and bat, and play ball with me." Joey's eyes sparkled. "And take me to Yankee Stadium to see Joe DiMaggio –"

"Joey, stop!" Mrs. Webster grabbed his arm. Concern showed in her brown eyes. "Don't go counting your chickens. We don't know what the news is. I don't want you getting your hopes up –"

He wiggled free. "I can't wait to see him. My daddy! My daddy's comin'!"

Smiling, he all but floated down the hall to the bathroom to wash the blood off his face.

MISS E. MACNEILL
ORPHANS' SERVICES
BOROUGH OF BRONX
CITY OF NEW YORK

announced gold letters that wobbled over waves of smoky glass in the office door.

Joey hated that word. *Orphan.* A child with no mother or father. No family. Always before, when he'd come to Miss MacNeill's office, it had made him feel lonely and scared.

But not today. Today, standing beside Mrs. Webster, as tidy as her neat stitches could mend his shirt, as clean as her vigorously applied washcloth could scrub his ears, as presentable as he could be with a split lip, he could look right at that word and laugh. He was no orphan!

Why, he thought with a shock, *my daddy might be in Miss MacNeill's office right now!* Yes, he imagined, his mind racing, when Miss MacNeill had finally got hold of his daddy, he was so anxious to be reunited with his long-lost son that he'd hopped on the first train and was, at this very moment, pacing the floor, waiting for him.

Joey raised his hand to knock.

"Take your cap off before you go in a lady's office," Mrs. Webster whispered.

Joey snatched off his New York Yankees cap and stuffed it in his back pocket, then knocked. At Miss MacNeill's cheery "Come in," he burst into the office and looked around.

His father wasn't there. The room was empty – except for the usual desk and filing cabinet, the geranium on the windowsill, the stack of folders, the New York cityscape on the wall. Miss MacNeill, looking summery in a pale yellow blouse and straight brown skirt, came around her desk to greet them with a smile.

"Mrs. Webster, Joey, hello." She motioned. "Please, have a seat."

"Where is he?"

"Who?"

"Guess he couldn't get here that fast. When's he coming?"

"*Who?*"

"My daddy."

"Your daddy?"

"You found him, didn't you?"

Miss MacNeill hesitated and looked away. "I think you'd better sit down, Joey."

Joey placed his hands on his hips. "Not till I know where my daddy is."

Mrs. Webster yanked him by the arm. "You sit down when Miss MacNeill tells you to, and don't give her any sass." He sat. Glared.

Miss MacNeill circled around behind her desk, sat down, opened a folder, closed it. "Joey . . . I'm afraid I have very sad news." She paused. "Well, there's no good way to put this, Joey. I finally tracked your father down to Newark, New Jersey. He . . . died . . . about a year ago. There was . . . an incident in a barroom and he and another man were —"

"No!" Joey jumped to his feet. "You're lying!"

Dead! Not his daddy, too. Now he really *was* an orphan. The strong arms that he'd imagined holding him vanished. The shiny car. The home in Chicago . . .

"There's more, I'm afraid," Miss MacNeill went on. "Your grandparents, your father's parents, have also passed away. They were living in Kansas City, but a car accident took them three years ago."

Grandparents. As soon as she said it, a memory arose in Joey, one that had been buried for years. Two black faces smiling down at him, warm arms holding him against a soft chest, mingled smells of lilacs and starch and hair oil.

"What a shame," Mrs. Webster said, shaking her head. "They were good folks, your grandmama and grand-daddy, Joey. You know, they wanted to take you when your mama and daddy started . . . going downhill. But your parents wouldn't let them."

They'd wanted him.

But they were dead. So that possibility, only just remembered, was gone. Tears started to Joey's eyes. He clenched his teeth not to cry.

Mrs. Webster rose, enfolding him in her arms.

He jerked away. "Leave me alone."

Then it hit him. Newark. That was only over the bridge in New Jersey. His grandparents had an excuse, but his daddy had been living right nearby all those years, and he'd never got in touch with him and Mama, never come to see them. Never played with his son, never helped out during the bad times, when Mama was shoot-ing the drug into her arm. His daddy hadn't cared. Not about Mama. Not about him.

"I hate him!" His fist flailed out and knocked over a can of pencils on Miss MacNeill's desk. The pencils clat-tered to the floor. Joey wished he could break every one.

He wished he could find his daddy and kill him all over again. "I'm glad he's dead."

"Joseph Sexton, how can you say such a thing!" Mrs. Webster scolded.

Joey tossed his head. "He didn't care about me. Why should I care about him? Now I got no family –"

"But Joey, you do!" Miss MacNeill broke in.

Joey looked up. Miss MacNeill was smiling. "That's why I called you here. I wanted to tell you right away, but . . . Please sit down."

Joey sat, feeling a shiver of excitement.

Miss MacNeill riffled through the papers in the file. "When the police released your mother's things a few weeks ago, there was a bundle of papers, including her birth certificate. And guess what, Joey – her maiden name wasn't Green, as we thought, but Greenberg. And I've found your mother's family – her father, sister, and niece – alive and well and living in Brooklyn. Isn't that wonderful?"

Mama's family! Joey never knew Mama had any family. Why . . . they'd be *his* family. He had one after all! For a moment, hope flared in his chest.

Then it died right down. "Greenberg?" he said suspiciously. "How come Mama never told me her name was Greenberg? How come she changed her name?"

"I don't know."

"How come she never talked about them? How come they never came to see us?"

Miss MacNeill looked serious. "I don't know, Joey. I'm sure there were reasons." She brightened. "But that's not important right now. The important thing is, I spoke to your grandfather, Mr. Sam Greenberg, and to your aunt, Mrs. Frieda Rosen – she's your mother's older sister, Joey. She's a widow; her husband died in the war. And she's very anxious to meet you and welcome you into their home."

Welcome you into their home.

Mama's sister. His aunt. His grandfather. He hadn't even known they existed.

"A girl?" he said. "The kid?"

Miss MacNeill consulted her notes. "Yes. Roberta, her name is, and she's your age, Joey. Just turned ten in April. A couple of months older than you."

"Won't that be nice, a cousin to play with?" Mrs. Webster said.

Joey snorted. "Who wants to play with some girl? She's probably all prissy, like the girls in my class. Rather have a boy."

"Even so, isn't it swell to discover a cousin you never knew you had?" Miss MacNeill said.

It was, though Joey wasn't going to admit it. *Maybe,* he thought, *if this Roberta isn't too girly-girly, I could teach her how to play baseball.*

"You know, Joey," Mrs. Webster said, "your mama's people is white folks. Might be easier for you to get along."

That might be true, too, Joey thought. *Couldn't be worse, anyway.* He was sick of being picked on by Jerome and the other Negroes. Sick of being called names. Sick of being left out of games. Once, his friend Harry, one of the other mixed-race kids, had said to him, "You're lucky, Joey. You could pass." Meaning, pass for white. Joey supposed Harry was right. His skin was a creamy light brown, not much darker than Mama's. His black hair sprang into thick curls, but not the kinky, all-over mat of a Negro. His nose was a little broader than a white's, a little flatter; his lips a little fuller. But stand him next to Jerome, and he looked white. Sure he did. Why else would the Negroes call him *whitebread*? If he could fit into a white neighborhood . . .

He grunted. "Guess so."

Miss MacNeill smiled. "Good. I'll get back to your aunt right away." She tapped a pen thoughtfully on her fingers. "Funny . . . they seemed surprised to hear about you, Joey —"

"What do you mean, surprised?"

"Well . . . they didn't seem to know about you. But –"

"Didn't know about me! Why the heck not?"

"You watch your mouth," Mrs. Webster warned.

"Didn't know – or just didn't care?"

"Joseph Sexton, you mind how you talk about your mama's people," Mrs. Webster scolded.

"Why should I? They never did anything for Mama and me."

Miss MacNeill leaned forward. "Joey, I know it seems strange that your relatives didn't know about you. There seems to have been a lack of communication between your mother and her family, a misunderstanding of some sort. But honestly, your aunt was very excited. She said she couldn't wait to see you."

Joey didn't answer. Something had been niggling around in the back of his mind, and now he knew what it was. *She* couldn't wait to see you. *She* was anxious to welcome you. *She* was eager to have you come.

He looked straight at Miss MacNeill. "What about him?"

Miss MacNeill flushed. "What do you mean, Joey?"

"You said my aunt was excited. What about my grand-father?"

Miss MacNeill shuffled some papers on her desk. "Well . . . we spoke at length, and he . . . was willing to have you come."

Joey saw right through that. "He doesn't want me."

"Now, Joey, I didn't say that."

"You didn't have to." He looked at Miss MacNeill's flushed face. "What's going on?"

Miss MacNeill hesitated. Then she said, "All right, Joey, I'll give it to you straight. Your grandfather was a little unsure about this. It wasn't that he didn't want you —" She put up a hand as Joey started to speak. "He just wasn't sure if it would work out. He said you could come. And as long as you behave yourself, you can stay."

"What!" Joey jumped to his feet. "It's like a test? If I'm bad, I get kicked out?"

"I wouldn't put it that way."

"I don't have to prove anything to anybody! I don't need him! I can take care of myself."

Mrs. Webster grabbed his arm and pulled him down. "Now, you stop that foolishness. You should be grateful. Here's family that's willing to take you in —"

"Well, I don't want to be took in by them."

"You've got no choice, mister, and I suggest you button your lip so's they don't change their mind."

"Let 'em. I don't care."

But even as he said it, he knew Mrs. Webster was right. Mama was dead. His daddy was dead. His daddy's parents were dead. He couldn't stay with Mrs. Webster. Even though she'd been kind to him — and he'd never admit it, but she *had* been kind, taking him in, letting him cry and rage those first few weeks, patching up his cuts and scrapes, putting up with his fighting and sassing – she was too sickly and poor to care for him. That left a foster home. Or, worse, an orphanage. Away . . . alone . . . with no one who loved him. . . . No, it was too terrifying to think about.

So he was stuck – with relatives who didn't want him.

Miss MacNeill came around the side of her desk and took Joey's hands. "Joey, this is a wonderful chance for you. A new family, a new start. Surely it's not too hard for you to be a good boy, is it?"

"Well . . ."

"You do manage to behave once in a while, don't you?"

Joey chuckled. "Yeah."

"Not too often," Mrs. Webster teased.

"Hey!"

Miss MacNeill smiled. "It'll work out, Joey, you'll see. They're family, after all."

Joey grunted. It still rankled. *Behave or else.* But maybe Miss MacNeill was right. They *were* family. Mama's family.

"All right," he said. "I'll try."

"Attaboy," Miss MacNeill said, and Mrs. Webster patted his hand.

Miss MacNeill spoke to Mrs. Webster, making arrangements, then turned back to him. "It's settled, then, Joey. Mrs. Webster will pack up your things and bring you down here on Monday. Then I'll take you over to meet your new family in Brooklyn."

Joey was tugging his Yankees cap over his black curls when it hit him.

"Brooklyn!" he said in disgust. "That's Dodgers territory. I'm goin' to live with Dodgers fans in Brooklyn!"

3

Walking beside Miss MacNeill down a tree-lined street in Brooklyn, Joey clutched a battered suitcase that Mrs. Webster had packed for him.

He'd actually choked up saying goodbye to the old lady. When she'd wept, he'd had to rub something out of his own eye. Then she'd said, "Now you behave yourself, you hear?" and he'd replied, "You ain't the boss of me," and felt much better.

Now, though, he was too busy checking out his new neighborhood to think about Mrs. Webster. When he and Miss MacNeill had stepped off the streetcar at Utica Avenue, it had been like stepping into a new world. Compared to Courtlandt Avenue up in the Bronx, Utica Avenue was busy and rich-looking. New Studebakers, DeSotos, and Fords rumbled past on either side of the streetcar tracks. Stores sported new red-and-white striped

awnings and crisp, clean signs. GROSSMAN'S CHIL-
DREN'S WEAR, said one, and the window was full of frilly
dresses and sharp-looking shorts sets. FELDMAN'S TOYS
had jumpropes and roller skates and dolls piled high.
The sidewalks were swept clean. There were no piles of
garbage, no smell of pee in the alleys. . . .

But what was most amazing to Joey was the sea of
white faces. Men, women and children, old and young, all
white. A few people looked at him curiously, but no one
seemed bothered. Maybe he *would* fit in.

Miss MacNeill paused in front of a drugstore called
Gershon's. "I need some chewing gum, Joey. Do you
mind?"

Inside was a newsstand. "I'll wait for you here." While
Miss MacNeill went to the candy counter, he picked up a
Brooklyn newspaper and turned to the sports section. In
the bustle of getting ready the day before, he hadn't heard
the Yankees' score.

"Jackie Robs Pirates' Ace with Ninth Inning Homer,"
read the headline. Jackie Robinson, of course. You didn't
have to be a Dodgers fan to know who that was. Joey
scanned the opposite page. "Robinson Notches Twelfth
Stolen Base." *Man, that guy is fast*, Joey thought. All those
people who'd said a Negro would never make it in the
major leagues – bet they were eating their words now.
Black, white, or purple – Jackie was showing them that it

wasn't color that mattered, it was skill. And boy, did he have it.

Joey scanned down the page. "Brooklyn Skipper: 'Jackie's Got the Goods.'" "Robinson Says Scare Tactics Won't Stop Him." Cripes, enough already. He turned the page. There, finally –

A voice behind him said, "Yanks Double Red Sox, 6-3."

Joey whirled. "Miss MacNeill! You scared me."

"Checking the score?"

"Yeah." Joey folded the newspaper and put it back on the rack. Following her out of the store he added disgustedly, "They hardly even report Yankees news here. Everything's Robinson, Robinson, Robinson."

"Don't you like Jackie Robinson?" she asked.

"Sure I do. He's fantastic. I wish he was on the Yankees. But he's a Dodger."

"That makes him the enemy, does it?"

"Of course." Joey eyed her suspiciously. "Aren't you a Yankees fan?"

"You bet. Bronx girl, through and through. But I wonder . . . now that you're living in Brooklyn –"

"Forget it!" Joey said. "Nothing could make me stop rooting for the Yankees."

"All right, Joey –"

"They could torture me. Pull out my fingernails. Burn me at the stake. I'll never be for the Dodgers."

"I don't think your new family has torture in mind," Miss MacNeill said.

"They better not," Joey said darkly.

They turned down a side street. Here there were homes, and instead of the soot-darkened apartments of his old neighborhood, these were stately row houses of dark red brick. And there were patches of grass, shady trees, clusters of purple and yellow petunias edging walkways and fringing window boxes. An ice-cream wagon bell clanged from a side street, followed by the excited chatter of children looking to buy an Italian ice on this sweltering day.

Men in straw boaters hurried by. Women in housedresses and straw sun hats pushed baby carriages. On stoops and front walks, girls cradled dolls, colored, played hopscotch. Little boys with red neckerchiefs darted behind shrubs, popping up to shoot each other with imaginary guns. "Got you, Injun! You're dead!"

Families. . . .

No. Forget it. He wasn't part of any family yet. And if he stepped out of line, he'd be out on his ear. No point getting his hopes up.

But he couldn't help it. Maybe his grandfather would play ball with him . . . or take him fishing. And his aunt – would she look like Mama? Would she bake cookies? Tuck him in at night? And his cousin – even though she was a girl, maybe she wouldn't be too bad. Maybe she'd even be a friend. . . .

Idiot! It wasn't going to happen. His family hadn't wanted him for the last ten years. They weren't going to now.

But they were *taking him in. Surely that meant something.* And what if they lived in a nice brick house like that one across the street, with a pot of pansies on each step? Maybe it would even be big enough for him to have his own room, instead of sleeping on the couch. Wouldn't that be something!

He snapped out of it as he and Miss MacNeill crossed Schenectady Avenue, then continued onto Crown Street. Miss MacNeill paused in front of a row house and checked the number against a paper in her hand. "Here we are," she said cheerfully, and started up the walk.

Joey stopped dead. It was too soon. He wasn't ready. He was dying of curiosity. He didn't want to meet them. He wanted to run away. He longed to see them.

He ran to catch up, taking the steps two at a time.

Footsteps sounded. The knob turned. The door opened.

She was so like Mama, Joey started. Older, fairer, softer, rounder, the cleft in her chin only a dimple, not a deep ridge like Mama's and his. But the brown eyes and the full-lipped mouth were just the same. Put them side by side and you'd know in an instant they were sisters.

I'm not going to cry.

Staring at him, she gasped. Joey froze, instantly wary. But a moment later her hand leaped to her heart and her eyes flooded with tears. "Oh my God – Joseph?"

Miss MacNeill held out her hand. "Mrs. Rosen?"

"Forgive me, you must be Miss MacNeill. It's just that he –" To Joey, "– that you – oh, Joseph!" She gathered Joey in her arms.

She was warm and she smelled like roses and she was holding him like she'd never let go. Joey could feel her heart pounding against his shoulder. For a moment, his beat wildly in rhythm and he melted against her.

She broke off with a laugh. "Excuse me! What am I thinking, keeping you out there on the doorstep? Please, come in, come in."

Joey and Miss MacNeill stepped into a narrow hallway. Behind his aunt, running footsteps pounded, then stopped short. Joey peered around her. A girl. About his age. A little taller. Slim. Very short, curly, dark hair. Round brown eyes. Full lips. Swarthy skin – not as creamy-brown as his, more olive, like some Italian kids he knew.

She looks like me, Joey thought with a shock. *I look like her.*

Hands on hips, she was staring at him. Glaring, actually. "You play ball?"

"Yeah."

"Can you hit?"

"Yeah." What was this?

"Field?"

"Yeah!"

"All right, then."

Joey fumed. Just who did she think she was, grilling *him* about baseball? Okay, so now that he looked, he saw that she did have on Keds, the white canvas scuffed to a satisfying gray-brown. And she did have scabs on her knees. So she wasn't completely girly-girly. But still, where did she get off?

"Roberta, where are your manners?" His aunt turned to Miss MacNeill. "I'm sorry, Miss MacNeill. My daughter, Roberta."

"Hello, Miss MacNeill," the girl said, finally looking at the social worker.

"How do you do, Roberta?"

"And your cousin. Joseph Sexton. My daughter, Roberta."

The girl grimaced. Turning to Joey, she snapped, "Don't ever call me that. I'm Bobbie."

"All right! And don't you dare call me Joseph. I'm Joey."

His aunt ruffled his hair. "Joey, is it?" She smiled. "Then you must call me Aunt Frieda. That's who I am, after all."

He looked up. "Okay . . . Aunt Frieda." The words felt strange in his mouth. He'd never called anyone aunt before.

Aunt Frieda motioned down the hall. "Please, come in, let's go in the living room. Make yourselves comfortable. Let me get you a cold drink. You must be parched, such a hot day. . . ." She led them down the hallway. Directly ahead, a flight of steps, dark wood with red carpet runners, led upstairs from the end of the hall. On the left was a dining room. A square table of honey-hued, gleaming wood stood in the middle of the room, and brightly colored paintings – a sailboat tilting in the wind, a country cottage surrounded by willows – hung on the walls. Beyond the dining room was the kitchen, the floor a checkerboard of big black-and-white squares. A fresh lemony smell wafted out.

It's so tidy, Joey thought. *Such a nice place to live.*

Then it hit him. This was Mama's house! She had grown up here! How strange it was to imagine her as a baby, a little girl, a teenager, in these very rooms.

His aunt turned to the right, into a long, narrow living room. Along one long wall was a tan-colored couch with curvy wooden arms; on the opposite wall, a fireplace, its mantel crowded with framed photographs. At the back end of the living room there was a door to another room, now closed. Facing onto the street was a big bay window.

In front of it was a large console radio on a small table.

Then Joey saw him. In the flurry of meeting his aunt and cousin, of seeing the house, he'd forgotten all about him. Now, rising to his feet from an armchair near the window, was a man. His grandfather. Mama's daddy.

He wasn't big, medium build, but he gave the impression of tallness. Back straight, head high, arms straight at his sides. His hair, steel-gray still flecked with black, waved back thickly from a high forehead. Mama – God, he looked like Mama. The deep cleft in the chin. The dark eyes. They were on him at once, those eyes.

Shock. Joey saw it on his grandfather's face. The old man's body seemed to tense, though he didn't move a muscle.

Joey's heart sank.

But in the next moment, though he still hadn't moved, his grandfather's body seemed to soften. His eyes turned liquid, pools of warm brown shining at him.

Joey stood there, confused.

"Oh, Daddy," Aunt Frieda said, her voice breaking, "isn't he just the image of Becky?"

A long pause. Then, "Yes," he bit off harshly.

There was an awkward silence. Aunt Frieda started edging out of the room. "I'll . . . uh . . . get that lemonade now. Excuse me."

Another moment of stillness. Joey's grandfather settled back into his chair by the window, Bobbie in a matching chair facing his. Miss MacNeill sat on the couch, Joey beside her.

Somebody say something, Joey thought, and finally, Miss MacNeill did. "What a lovely home, Mr. Greenberg. Have you lived here long?"

"Thirty-six years. Since Frieda was a baby. We raised our . . . our children here, my wife and I. She died, almost thirteen years ago."

"I'm sorry."

He lifted his hand in acknowledgment, then let it fall. "I was going to sell the house once Frieda married and moved out – after all, what did I need a big house for? But somehow I never got around to it. And it all worked out in the end, because after Manny died – that was Frieda's husband – she and Bobbie had someplace to come, they shouldn't be alone."

Miss MacNeill looked at Bobbie. "That must have been very hard for you, Bobbie, losing your daddy."

Bobbie nodded.

"How old were you?"

"Seven. But he went overseas when I was four. I can hardly remember him."

Like me, Joey thought.

Bobbie took a framed picture from the mantel and brought it to Miss MacNeill. "That's him," she said. Joey looked over Miss MacNeill's shoulder. A man in an Army Air Corps uniform, wavy hair beneath his pointed cap, big grin, crinkles around the eyes.

Miss MacNeill smiled up at Bobbie. "He looks nice."

"Yeah." Bobbie sighed, taking the picture back. "I miss him."

And suddenly Joey remembered. A picture of Mama, taken about four years ago, during one of her good times. She hadn't looked so great in her bad times — hair unwashed, skin pale, collarbones sticking out because she forgot to eat. But this picture had been taken when she was off the drugs, and she looked so pretty, with a big smile and her dimples showing. It had sat on her dresser, with her perfume bottles and lipsticks. He wondered what had happened to it. *Must have gotten overlooked when Mrs. Webster was packing up Mama's things.* He felt a pang, wishing he had that picture.

But there must be other pictures of Mama here, Joey thought, scanning the photographs on the mantel. There was a fat baby in a bonnet — Bobbie, he guessed. A wedding picture, in which he recognized his aunt as the young bride. An older couple — the man was a younger version of his grandfather, so the woman must be his grandmother. Bobbie on a tricycle. Aunt Frieda in front of a shiny sedan, her arms full of flowers.

No pictures of Mama. *Why not?*

Joey's aunt came back in, carrying a tray, and handed around glasses. Everyone sipped. The lemonade was delicious and Joey wanted to down it all in one gulp, but he made it last. You never knew when there was going to be more.

"Mrs. Rosen, I think you said you work in a law office?" Miss MacNeill said.

Joey's aunt flapped her hand. "I'm just a secretary."

"Not just!" Bobbie protested. She turned to Miss MacNeill. "Mr. Turchin – that's Mama's boss – said she's the best secretary he's ever had."

"Bobbie!" Aunt Frieda said, mortified.

"Well, he did."

Joey hated to admit it, but he liked the way his cousin stuck up for her mama.

"And Mr. Greenberg, what do you do?" Miss MacNeill asked.

"I'm retired. Was in the printing business for forty years. Now that Frieda's gone back to work full-time, I look after the house, do the marketing, take care of Bobbie."

"And now you'll have Joey, too," Miss MacNeill said.

Another pause. "Yes."

"You turned ten in April, right, Bobbie?" Miss MacNeill said.

"Right."

"And Joey had his tenth birthday a couple of weeks ago." To Aunt Frieda she said, "Isn't it nice how close they are in age? Did you and your sister realize your babies were only two months apart?"

His aunt colored, gripping her lemonade glass. "Uh . . . no. I mean, we knew . . . that is, I was expecting Bobbie at the time, and I knew that my sister was expecting, too. But we had no idea about Joey –"

Her father shot her a look and she broke off.

What's going on? Joey thought.

"Yes, I've been meaning to ask you," Miss MacNeill said. "When we spoke, you didn't seem to know about Joey. It's odd, isn't it, what with you living here and your sister just up in the Bronx."

A look passed between Joey's aunt and grandfather. Then she stammered, "Well, uh . . . we weren't in touch. You see, she left and . . . we didn't hear, and . . ." A stricken look crossed her face. ". . . and the years went by. Maybe we should have tried to keep in touch, but –"

"She made her bed and she had to lie in it."

"But Daddy," Aunt Frieda said, her face reddening, "maybe if we'd –"

Joey's grandfather slammed his glass down on the small table. "That's enough."

Sounds of sipping. Throats clearing. "Well," Miss MacNeill said into the silence, "this must be a very happy day for you."

"Yes . . . yes, it is," his aunt said.

"I only wish it hadn't taken a tragedy for your family to be reunited."

Aunt Frieda's eyes filled with tears. "Thank you, Miss MacNeill."

"I was sorry to be the one to bring you the sad news," Miss MacNeill added. "But what a stroke of luck to find you."

"Yes . . . how *did* you find us?"

"Well, after – after I received Joey's case, I started looking for his family. I tracked down his father, Mr. Horace Sexton, only to find out that he had . . . passed away. Then I came upon your – Mrs. Sexton's birth certificate, and discovered that her maiden name was Greenberg."

His aunt looked puzzled. "What else would it have been?"

"Well, she'd been using the name Green. Rebecca Green Sexton. So we thought –"

"Green? She changed her name?" Joey's grandfather said sharply.

Aunt Frieda put her hands to her cheeks. "My God, she must have –"

"You see?" the old man snapped. "She didn't want us."

How does he know? Joey thought angrily. *He has no idea what Mama wanted.*

His aunt began, "Oh no, Daddy, I don't believe that –"

"Go on, Miss MacNeill," his grandfather interrupted.

"Uh . . . where was I?" Miss MacNeill stammered. "Oh, yes, Greenberg. So then it was a matter of going through all the Greenbergs in Brooklyn. Let me tell you, that was no easy task," she added with a chuckle. "Luckily, Mrs. Webster didn't mind keeping Joey a little longer –"

"Mrs. Webster?"

"Oh, I thought I told you about her. She's your sister's neighbor. She lived across the hall. After . . . the death – I don't know how long afterward, I gather Joey was on his own for a day or so before Mrs. Webster took him in –"

"On his own?" Joey's grandfather said, looking shocked. "All alone?"

"It was only two days," Joey said defensively. "I was used to it anyway. I can take care of myself."

"Used to it!" A pained look, followed by an angry flush. "She was not a fit mother."

"Daddy . . ." Aunt Frieda soothed.

"Don't you say that about Mama!"

"Joey!" Miss MacNeill gasped.

38

"How would *you* know, anyway?"

"Joseph!" His aunt's hands flew to her face.

"You never bothered to come –"

"Silence!" his grandfather roared.

"Joey, you mustn't speak like that to your grandfather," said Miss MacNeill.

"You impertinent hellion!"

"Joey, apologize," Miss MacNeill said. "Right now."

Joey sat, teeth clenched.

They were all waiting.

"Sorry," Joey muttered in a barely audible voice. His only satisfaction was that he didn't mean it.

A heavy silence.

"Well, I –" Aunt Frieda stammered.

"I think . . ." Miss MacNeill said, "I really should be going. I must get back to the office." She stood, smoothing her skirt. "Nice to meet you, Mr. Greenberg, Mrs. Rosen." She rested a hand on Bobbie's shoulder. "I'm so glad Joey will have a friend." She turned to Joey. "Wait for me by the front door."

"But –"

"By the front door."

Joey started down the hallway.

"I don't know about this," he heard his grandfather say.

Joey stopped. A cold band squeezed his heart.

"Now, Daddy, it's just a little rough patch," his aunt soothed.

"I'm sure it'll work out, Mr. Greenberg," Miss MacNeill said.

Joey didn't hear his grandfather's reply, but when nothing happened, he supposed he wasn't getting thrown out. Yet.

The band released. Relief washed over him.

He quickly pushed it away as Miss MacNeill's heels clicked sharply down the hallway. She stopped in front of him, hands on hips. "Now, you listen, young man –"

"That wasn't my fault!"

"If you hadn't opened a fresh mouth –"

"He started it."

"He's your grandfather, Joey. You must show respect."

"Not if he talks about Mama that way."

"Joey, you've *got* to behave." she said sharply. She took his chin in her hand. More softly she said, "Please, Joey. Try. You can do it."

But what if I can't? he thought.

Miss MacNeill knelt, hugged him. And then she was gone.

4

Joey's spirits lifted as he followed Bobbie upstairs. To the right, at the top of the steps, was Aunt Frieda's room. Joey caught a glimpse of a yellow and green flowered bedspread as he passed by. Directly across from the staircase, at the back of the house, was a bathroom, its floor and walls tiled in white with a zigzag pattern of black around the edges. Fresh white towels hung on racks. On the left, at the back, was Bobbie's room. *At least*, Joey thought, glancing in, *there are no dolls on the bed.*

Finally Bobbie led him to a small room at the front of the house, next to hers. "This is your room," she said.

Joey stood in the doorway, gripping his suitcase. He hardly dared to believe it, though he'd dreamed of it for days.

"Aren't you going to go in and unpack?" Bobbie asked.

That bossy voice again. "Yeah," he tossed back.

"You want to go out and play after?"

"Yeah."

"Okay. I'll change and come get you."

She left. Carefully, Joey put the suitcase on the bed and turned to survey his room. It was small, maybe ten steps in each direction. A dormer window faced the street, with a wide sill that was perfect for resting your elbows on. Quilt with blue-and-white overlapping circles on the bed. Small, dark brown dresser with a doily on top. Wooden arm chair. Small closet. Clean smell of furniture polish.

His room. *His* place. At the apartment, he'd shared a room with Mama, or when she was too messed up, slept on the sofa. Now he had his own room. His own dresser. He could put his things where he wanted. Not that he had so many. Just what was in the suitcase.

He clicked open the latches, quickly stripped off his "school clothes" – black-and-white checked shirt and black trousers, both still stiff from Mrs. Webster's starch, and brown oxfords – and put on a striped T-shirt, shorts, and his comfortable old Keds.

That left some underwear and socks, a pair of pajamas, a couple of T-shirts, and a pair of dungarees. This was the sum total of his clothing, or at least those items that Mrs. Webster had deemed worth keeping. She hadn't made him go back into the apartment, not after he'd come home that terrible day and found Mama slumped on the floor, a vacant look in her unseeing eyes. Mrs. Webster said he'd seen enough, more than enough for one boy, and had gone herself to sort through Mama's things, pack up Joey's few decent clothes, and empty the refrigerator.

Now, Joey put his clothes away, opening and closing his dresser drawers with pleasure. Even though the dresser was small, his clothes took up barely half the space. He took out his baseball glove, threw the doily into a drawer, and put his glove in its place.

Finally, all that remained in the suitcase were his most prized possessions. His Yankees baseball cap. His Yankees baseball cards. His Yankees photos. His Yankees newspaper clippings.

He jammed the cap on his head, then surveyed the room, wondering where to put the rest. His eye fell on a bulletin board hanging on the wall beside the window. There were even some thumbtacks stuck in it. Perfect.

Right at the center, in the place of honor, Joey stuck his Joe DiMaggio baseball card. Above the card he tacked a picture of DiMaggio that he'd clipped out of the paper just the other day, the bat swinging around, the powerful shoulders twisted, the head lifted, watching as the ball soared. Below it, another photo of DiMaggio, this time leaping for a catch at center, his arm straight up over his head, his feet extended beneath him. There was a small grease spot on DiMaggio's arm – Mama had been about to use the sports section to drain fried potatoes, and Joey had rescued it just in time. He'd made her promise never again to drip grease on anything to do with the Yankees. The Dodgers, okay. The Yankees, never. She'd given him her word.

To the right of the DiMaggio card, Joey tacked a recent article about the Yankees' winning season – "Yanks Notch 38th Win of Campaign," was the headline; to the left, the 1947 New York Yankees team picture, the names smudged from running his finger over them so many times. Around the outside edges, he placed his other baseball cards. Allie Reynolds, rearing back in pitching motion . . . Yogi Berra, cradling the catcher's mask against his chest . . . Snuffy Stirnweiss, bat cocked over his shoulder . . . Phil Rizzuto . . . Spec Shea . . .

At last Joey stood back to admire his work. It was a shrine, that's what it was. And never was there a team that deserved it more.

He closed and latched the suitcase. It still felt heavy, but a quick look showed that there was nothing left inside. He stashed it in the closet.

A knock sounded at the door.

"You ready?" Bobbie's voice called.

"Yeah."

She came in. The blouse and skirt were gone. In their place, a red polo shirt, white shorts, and a blue baseball cap with a white *B*.

Joey stared at the Dodgers cap. She stared at his Yankees cap, then looked past him to the bulletin board. "Yankees!" Her cheeks colored. "You can't put up Yankees stuff in here!"

"Why not?"

"'Cause!"

"'Cause why?"

"'Cause . . . this is Brooklyn. Dodgers territory."

Joey put his hands on his hips. "So? It's a free country. I can root for whoever I want."

"Not in Brooklyn!"

"I'm from the Bronx and I root for the Bronx Bombers."

"You're from Brooklyn now. You got to root for the Dodgers."

"Never!" He tossed his head. "Besides, why would I want to root for that bunch of losers?"

Her finger stabbed his chest. "You take that back!"

He scoffed. "The Dodgers always lose."

Her face turned red. "That's not true. We're doing better this year —"

"Ha! The Yanks have won ten World Series. How many have the Dodgers won?"

Bobbie went silent.

"Zero. Zilch. None."

"Oh, shut up."

"Truth hurts."

"Listen, bud, if you live in Brooklyn, you better be for Brooklyn. And you better get rid of that Yankees cap —"

"Forget it! I *ain't* gonna take down my pictures and I *ain't* gonna take off my cap and I *ain't* gonna stop rooting for the New York Yankees. So there!"

They stood toe to toe, baseball caps touching.

Finally, Bobbie said through gritted teeth, "The only reason I'm puttin' up with you — the *only* reason — is 'cause you're my cousin. You got that?"

"Well, the only reason *I'm* puttin' up with *you* is 'cause you're *my* cousin."

They glared at each other.

"All right, let's go," Bobbie muttered.

Joey grabbed his glove, hoping Bobbie wouldn't notice how ratty it was. They crossed the room. Bobbie turned in the doorway. "You're gonna get the stuffing beat out of you in that cap."

"I don't care."

She shrugged. "Don't come running to me when the bullies start in on you."

Joey's cheeks grew warm. "I ain't asking no girl to take care of me."

"Fine!"

"Fine!"

They pounded down the stairs. When they reached the bottom, Bobbie called around the banister, "Zeyde, we're going out to play."

Joey didn't want to talk to her, the impossible, bossy loudmouth, but his curiosity got the better of him. "Who's Zeyde?"

She looked at him. "What do you mean, who's Zeyde? Zeyde's my grandpa. Your grandpa."

Joey blushed. "What kind of name is that? Besides, I thought his name was Sam."

Bobbie looked stupefied. "It means grandfather – in Yiddish."

"What's Yiddish?"

She rolled her eyes. "Don't you know nothin'? Yiddish is a language. What Jews talk."

"Jews? You mean, you're Jewish?"

"You didn't know that?"

Joey bristled. "How'm I supposed to know? Miss MacNeill never said nothing about no Jews."

"Well, we are. You are."

"*What!*"

"You are, too. Your mama was Jewish, and in the Jewish religion, if your mama's Jewish, you're Jewish. So you better get used to it."

Your mama was Jewish. Even as she said it, distant memories floated up: Mama with a white kerchief over her dark curly hair, lighting candles, chanting some strange words he didn't understand. Mama cooking a big dinner and singing a funny song. Those must have been Jewish things, he realized now. But that was a long time ago. He couldn't have been more than two or three when the memories faded. *Must have been when Mama got into the drugs.*

Joey thought over his new-found status. "Do I have to do anything?"

"Being Jewish, you mean? Well, you got to say prayers and stuff. Those are in Hebrew, not Yiddish. That's another Jewish language. And you got to go to Hebrew school –"

"School? More school?"

Sympathy glinted in Bobbie's eyes. "Yeah. But only during the school year. You get the summer off."

"Whew."

"And sometimes you got to go to *schul* –"

"What? *Another* school?"

"Not school, *schul*. It's Yiddish. Means synagogue."

48

"What's synagogue?"

Bobbie rolled her eyes. "Cripes, don't they teach you anything in the Bronx? It's a temple. Where Jews pray."

Joey digested that. This religion was sounding like a lot of work.

"And you got to light Shabbas candles –"

Joey hated to ask. "What's that?"

Bobbie put on a martyred look. "I see I'm gonna have my hands full, showing you what's what."

"Don't do me any favors!"

"Okay, I won't!"

They glared at each other.

"You want to stand around all day asking questions, or you want to get going?"

"Get going!"

"Fine!"

"Fine!"

Bobbie poked her head into the hall closet and came out with a baseball, a bat, and two gloves. She held out the older-looking of the two. "You want to use this glove? It was my daddy's."

Joey flushed. "Nothing wrong with my glove!"

"I didn't say there was. Sheesh! Just thought you might like to try it, that's all."

Joey looked closely at her. She didn't appear to be making fun of him. He glanced at the glove. Holy cow. He clung to his pride for five seconds, then reached for it. "Okay," he said offhandedly, "just for a change."

Rawlings. Just seeing the fabled name stitched across the back sent a shiver up his spine. The glove was the color of wood that has weathered in the rain and wind, golden-brown turned a warm gray. It had the texture of aged leather, soft and supple. He slipped his hand inside. It was big, but still it felt as though his hand was made to go inside. The pocket pressed reassuringly against his palm. A thin band of webbing stretched protectively across the gap between the thumb and first finger. He lifted the glove to his face. It smelled of dirt and grass, sweat and sun.

Joey felt Bobbie's eyes on him. She was looking at him oddly, as if wondering why he was getting so carried away by a simple baseball glove.

"What?" he said defensively.

"Nothing."

"Fine."

"Fine."

As they walked down the street, Joey shot Bobbie a closer look. Her arms were wiry, her legs muscular. She moved easily, light on her feet. She carried the bat over her shoulder, her glove dangling from the tip. With her other hand, she tossed up the ball, caught it, tossed it, and caught it.

Who'da thunk it – a girl cousin who played baseball? Here he'd expected her to be all frilly and prissy, and instead she was a tomboy. What a stroke of luck!

Too bad she was a bossy, hot-headed, loudmouth know-it-all.

5

The playing field was a wide vacant lot, reddish-brown dirt, a few tufts of grass, and a lone maple tree at the back that had somehow been left standing. On one side stood a new house, its bricks bright red, its yard still raw earth. On the other side, separated by a chain-link fence, rose a tall, yellow-brick factory with a sign that said, PURITY SOAP. WE KEEP BROOKLYN CLEAN. Grayish-white smoke hung suspended over the chimney as if it didn't have the energy to rise through the humid air into the sky.

Five or six boys were in the lot. A sandy-haired boy with sticking-out ears lobbed pitches to the batter, who hit every ball with a fast, level swing. A burly catcher crouched behind him, pounding the center of his glove, encouraging the pitcher to "Put it in 'ere," and another sandy-haired boy chased down the hits in near right field.

Along the third base line, two fellows threw grounders back and forth. One, a chubby redhead, lumbering clumsily after the ball, missed nearly every one, and had to chase them into the yard of the unfinished house. But the other, small and wiry, olive-skinned, quickly scooped up the ball each time, as if he were scooping up a handful of water.

Joey watched wistfully, enjoying the boys' easy patter, the smells of leather and dirt, the *thwack* as the ball hit the glove, the sharp *pop* as the bat connected with the ball. He admired the way the pitcher's leg kicked up before he released the ball, the easy skip the groundball-catching boy took before his arm whipped around to throw. *You could pass*, he remembered his friend Harry saying. No one had looked at him funny on the street. If only he could slip right in with these kids . . .

The redhead missed a grounder and the ball rolled toward the road. He went to retrieve it, stomping down the slight drop to the sidewalk.

"Oh – hiya, Bobbie."

She waved. "Hi, Grossie."

The others turned and smiled.

"Hey, Vito, Louie, Larry." She waved again.

Now Joey saw that two of the boys looked remark-ably alike. Both had the same skinny build, the same sticking-out ears. They were dressed alike, too, in rolled-up dungarees, brown T-shirts, navy Keds, and Brooklyn baseball caps. Must be twins.

Only the batter and the catcher didn't greet Bobbie. "What do *you* want, Rosen?" the batter said, not bothering to look at her.

"What do you think?" Bobbie said.

Now he turned. "No girls allowed."

"Why not?"

"'Cause I say so."

"Yeah, Eli says so. So scram," the catcher said, jerking his thumb. He was big and muscular. Blond hair stuck out like straw from beneath his cap.

"Aw, come on, Eli, let her play," the clumsy boy said.

The batter glared at him. "Who makes the rules around here, Grossman?"

"You do, Eli, but —"

"And just you remember it, Fatso." Eli rounded on Bobbie. "Go find some girls to play with."

"Girls around here don't play ball, and you know it," she grumbled.

"That's 'cause girls can't play."

"They can so!" Bobbie said. "I'm better than half the boys in Brooklyn!"

The wiry boy pointed toward the back of the field. "Yeah, Eli, last time she hit one past the tree. That's farther than you ever did."

The other kids snickered as an angry flush spread up Eli's face. The catcher leaned toward him. "You want me to get 'im, Eli?"

"Sure, Tommy. Teach 'im a lesson."

As the catcher advanced, the small boy stepped back, hands up. "Aw, never mind."

Eli and Tommy exchanged a smirk. Then Eli flicked his head at Joey. "Who's that?"

"My cousin. Joey Sexton."

Eli took a step closer, then stopped, eyes wide. "Yankees! What're you doing with a Yankees cap?"

"Told you," Bobbie whispered.

"It's a free country," Joey said.

"Not in Brooklyn," Eli said. "Come on, Tommy." The pair advanced closer.

Then Eli stopped short. "Is this your idea of a joke, Rosen?"

"What?"

"He's not your cousin. Can't be."

"Why not?"

"'Cause he's a nigger!"

No! Joey's inner voice screamed. *Not them, too. Not here.*

"Watch your mouth," Bobbie said. "And for your information, Mister Smarty-pants, he is so my cousin. Just came to live with us. So there!"

"Guess you don't know everything, Fishkin," one of the twins said with a chuckle. But he clammed up when Tommy took a step toward him.

Eli glared at the two cousins. "Well, I don't care who he is. No nigger is playing in this field, and that's final."

"Don't call him that," Bobbie said. "Besides, Jackie Robinson's a Negro, and if he's good enough –"

"Yeah, and that's one too many in Brooklyn," Eli said. Tommy laughed.

Joey tensed. "What did you say?"

"I said, that's one nigger too many in Brooklyn. You got a problem with that, Nigger Boy?"

"I got Negro blood in me, and I ain't ashamed of it. But no one calls me *nigger*."

"I just did, Nigger."

"You take that back!" Joey didn't want to fight – especially on his first day in Brooklyn.

"N-n-n-nig –"

Joey jumped on him. Eli was a head taller. The move took him by surprise and he staggered as Joey's fist caught him in the chin.

"Holy cow!" somebody said.

"Why, you –" Eli recovered quickly. He grabbed Joey by the shirt and punched him in the nose.

"That's it, Eli," Tommy shouted.

Joey tasted blood. His fist plowed into Eli's stomach, but this time the bigger boy was ready and he hardly seemed to feel it. He returned the punch, hitting Joey in the eye. At the same time, Joey felt a ringing blow to the side of his head. Surprised, he turned. It was Tommy. Then he reeled as Eli caught him on the chin.

"Tommy Flanagan, you can't go two against one, you dirty fighter!" Bobbie shouted.

"Shut up, Rosen, you and your nigger cousin both."

"You take that back," Bobbie yelled, and to Joey's amazement she threw herself on Tommy. He stumbled and fell.

"Big tough Flanagan – knocked down by a girl," Vito hollered, and the others laughed.

That enraged Tommy further. He jumped to his feet, grabbed Bobbie by the arm and started hitting her.

She stuck up for me, Joey thought in amazement. A warm feeling swept over him, but it didn't last long. Another punch from Eli connected with his chin and put him on his backside.

"Give up, Nigger Boy?" Eli towered over him.

In answer, Joey rose to his feet, only to suffer a series of punches to the neck and arms. Out of the corner of a rapidly swelling eye, he saw Bobbie struggling gamely, but getting the worst of it from Tommy.

Another punch to his brow knocked Joey to his knees. He reached out with his foot, but Eli jumped out of the way. Joey was staggering to his feet when a voice shouted, "You boys! Cut it out or I'll call the cops!"

Everyone froze. A woman stood on the stoop of the new house, shaking her finger.

Eli let go of Joey. "Shoot," he said to Tommy, "that lady knows my mama. Come on, let's get out of here before she recognizes me." Eli and Tommy scooped up their gloves and bats and took off.

Hands on knees, panting, Joey and Bobbie watched them go. The others gathered around. "You okay, Bobbie?" the redhead asked.

"Yeah, Grossie," she said, wiping her face on her sleeve.

"You?" someone asked Joey.

He nodded, still winded.

"Those jerks," Louie said. "Calling Jackie Robinson a . . . that name."

"Aw, they're just a couple of dumbbells," Bobbie answered.

"You did good . . . both of you. Real good," Vito put in.

"Well . . . we better go," Grossie said.

"Yeah . . . better go," the others echoed.

"Sure. See ya, fellas," Bobbie said.

The boys gathered their things and left.

Joey took stock of himself. He could hardly see out of one eye. He felt wetness on his upper lip. He wiped his arm across his face and left a bloody streak on his forearm. His temple throbbed, and when he touched it gingerly, he winced at the pain.

Then he took a good look at his cousin. Her lower lip was bloody, there was a scratch across her forehead, the scab on her knee had torn off and was bleeding, and her shirt and shorts were filthy. She looked beautiful. Like a scrapper.

"Hey, thanks for . . . you know, coming in like that."

She blushed. "That's okay."

"No one ever did that for me."

"Well, you *are* my cousin. Besides, I can't stand it when guys fight dirty. It's just like Flanagan to gang up two against one. And just like Fishkin to call names."

Joey gave a harsh laugh. "In my old neighborhood they used to call me *whitebread. Cracker.* I fought about that, too."

She looked at him admiringly. "You're pretty tough."

"So're you."

They grinned at each other. Then Bobbie's smile faded. "Zeyde's gonna kill us," she said.

Fear seized Joey. The old man already had it in for him. "Aw, jeez, I didn't mean —"

"Don't worry, it wasn't your fault. It's just that Zeyde gets mad when I fight. Mama too."

"Those guys —"

"Fishkin started it. I'll tell them that. They'll understand."

"You think so?"

"Sure." She smiled. "Come on."

They picked up their stuff and started home. Joey knew he was in trouble. But right now he didn't care. His cousin had stood up for him. When push came to shove, she'd been on his side. No questions, no hesitation.

He had a friend.

Zeyde was in his chair by the window, listening to the radio. Bobbie motioned Joey to follow her on tiptoe down the hall, but they had only crept past the living-room doorway when a voice rang out. "Hold it."

They stopped.

"Come here."

They shot each other a look. Joey's heart pounded. They went into the living room and stood before their grandfather. His eyes flicked from one to the other, the color rising in his cheeks. Turning off the radio, he stood up.

"Zeyde, I can explain —" Bobbie began.

"I am ashamed."

"It wasn't our fault, Zeyde –"

"Roberta, you know better."

"It wasn't her fault . . . Zeyde," Joey put in, the word strange on his tongue. "She only came in when –"

"Silence!"

Aunt Frieda peeked in. "What's the matter?" Then, looking at the two children, "Oh, my goodness." Her hand flew to her mouth. "Bobbie!"

Zeyde pointed at Joey, his brows gathered into a thick black line. "Two minutes in this house and you disgrace us –"

"But Zeyde, it wasn't his fault," Bobbie argued.

"Bobbie, how could you?" Aunt Frieda twisted her apron in her hands. "You promised me you wouldn't fight anymore."

"I know, Mama, but I couldn't help it."

"And Joey," Aunt Frieda went on, tears welling up in her eyes, "you mustn't carry on like this."

"But Mama, they were calling him *nigger*."

"How terrible!"

"And then they ganged up, two against one."

Zeyde pointed at Joey. "So you dragged her into it?"

"No, I –"

"No, Zeyde, it wasn't like that –" Bobbie began.

"It's bad enough for you, young lady, carrying on like that when you know better. But *you!*" He pointed at Joey, his face crimson. "Running around like a wild thing, getting into fights, getting your cousin into mischief." He gestured toward the stairs. "Roberta, you stay in your room for an hour. And you, Joseph, don't show your face until suppertime."

"But Zeyde, that's not fair." Bobbie said.

"Daddy –" Aunt Frieda began.

He cut her off with a slash of the hand, then turned back to Joey and Bobbie. "Go!"

Wild thing . . . disgrace . . .

Joey's insides tightened. Had he blown it already? When he was allowed out of his room, would he be sent on his way?

At the top of the stairs, Bobbie gave his hand a squeeze and went into her room. Joey was about to go into the bathroom when he heard Zeyde say, "I told you that boy would be trouble, Frieda."

"Daddy, you wouldn't!"

"No. Not this time."

Joey let out a breath.

"Not that he doesn't deserve it –"

"But, Daddy, it wasn't really his fault. Such a cruel name those boys called him. No wonder he fought back. And maybe he hasn't been taught any better."

"That's no excuse."

"But it's not fair to punish one more than the other."

"Don't give me fair! We've got to be firm with that boy or he'll just get worse – and he'll be a bad influence on Bobbie. Not even one day here and he's got her brawling like a hoodlum. You want he should make her wilder than she already is?"

"No!"

"Well, he will, if we don't stop him."

"Oh, dear. Do you really think so, Daddy?"

"I know so. You let me handle this, Frieda."

There was a sigh. "Yes, Daddy."

Their footsteps went in opposite directions.

Joey stood there a moment, his hand gripping the top of the banister. Then he went into the bathroom and slammed the door. He should have known he wouldn't get a fair deal. His grandfather had it in for him. And his aunt knuckled under like a scared little mouse.

Instead of waiting to get kicked out, he should just leave now. Show them they couldn't treat him like this.

But where could he go?

Leaning on the sink, he regarded his bloodied face.

I told you that boy would be trouble.

Tears stung his eyes. Quickly he blinked them away.

Why should I cry?

But the tears spilled out anyway. He grabbed a cloth and pressed it to his face, whether to stop the blood or the tears, he didn't know.

6

The next day passed without incident. Joey and Zeyde stayed out of each other's way, and that was fine with Joey.

That night Bobbie set up a checkers board on the kitchen table and challenged Joey to a game. She was ahead, two games to one, and they were in the middle of the fourth game, when Aunt Frieda came into the kitchen. "All right, you two, put it away. Time for bed."

Joey ignored her, double-jumping Bobbie.

"Joey, did you hear me? I said put it away. It's bedtime." Aunt Frieda's voice was sharper this time.

Joey grinned at her. "You're kidding, right?"

"Why would I be kidding?"

Joey looked at Bobbie. "You got a bedtime?"

"Yeah. It's a little later in the summer, but —"

"Well, I don't. I always go to bed when I feel like it." He reached for Bobbie's men that he'd jumped.

Aunt Frieda folded the checkers board in half, scattering the pieces. "That's enough, Joey. It doesn't matter what you did before. In this house, you have a bedtime."

"I'm not going to bed in the middle of a checkers game!"

"Oh, yes you are."

Joey glanced at Bobbie. She didn't look the least bit upset. "That's no fair —"

"No," Aunt Frieda said firmly, "what's no fair is for you to stay up to all hours and then be tired and miserable the next day. Now, march."

Grumbling, Joey got up from the table. Bedtime! Of all the stupid things.

Aunt Frieda was just bossing him around because she didn't like him. Well, he wasn't too crazy about her, either.

A couple of days later, Aunt Frieda knocked on Joey's door to see if he had any clothes that needed washing. Busy rearranging his Phil Rizzuto and Spec Shea baseball cards, he called, "Yeah, I guess so."

Aunt Frieda poked her head in the door. "You want to give them to me, Joey? I'm ready to put in — Joey!"

"What?" He turned so quickly he nearly dropped the thumbtacks.

"Look at this room!"

Joey looked around the room. Bed, dresser, chair. "What?"

"What?" she repeated. "There are clothes everywhere! And your shoes, just kicked off and left. And your bed isn't made!"

"So?"

"It's a pigsty!"

Joey looked around again. All right, so he'd pretty much dropped his dirty clothes wherever he'd taken them off. What was the big deal?

Aunt Frieda put her hands on her hips. "Joseph Sexton, in this house we have rules."

"More rules!"

"Yes, and you're going to follow them. First of all, you're to make your bed every day –".

"What for? I'm just gonna sleep in it again –"

"And you put your dirty clothes in the laundry bag I gave you. And you put your shoes in the closet when you're not wearing them. And you pick up after yourself."

"I never had to do any of that stuff before –"

"I don't care. You're not going to live like a slob in this house. I want your dirty clothes – *in* the laundry bag – in five minutes. And you'll clean this room before you go out to play."

She left.

"You're picking on me," Joey called after her, but she didn't respond.

For crying out loud, he'd never heard of so many rules in his life.

That night when Joey came down for dinner, there was a platter of pot roast on the table, dark brown with fragrant juice pooling around it, a bowl of crisp green beans, a mound of rice, steaming like a small white volcano. And, in the center of the table, a basket of crusty rolls.

Everyone had just sat down at the table when Joey grabbed a roll and bit in.

"Joey!" Aunt Frieda and Zeyde said together.

He swallowed. "What?"

"You don't just grab like a heathen!" Zeyde said.

"What do you mean, *a heathen*?"

"Joey," Aunt Frieda said a little more gently, "it's not polite to take first. You pass the rolls and wait until others have helped themselves."

"Says who?"

"No manners," Zeyde grumbled.

"Well, no one ever told me," Joey said defensively. "And besides, what if there's none left by the time it gets to me?"

Aunt Frieda and Zeyde exchanged a sad look. What did *they* have to be sad about?

Aunt Frieda put her hand on his arm. "There's plenty, Joey. There's always more."

"There is?"

Another look. "Yes, Joey."

"Well . . . okay." Joey put the roll on his plate.

In bed, though, thinking about what Aunt Frieda had said earlier, Joey wasn't convinced. Everybody knew that the smartest thing was to take while you could get. How could you be sure there would always be more?

He climbed out of bed, tiptoed across his room and opened the door. All quiet. He crept down the stairs and into the kitchen. Silently, he opened the bread box and took out two rolls. Back upstairs, he tucked them under his pillow. He wasn't hungry, but just in case.

Three nights later, when his pillow was lumpy, he would find them, as hard as if they'd been fired in clay.

The next day was Friday, and all afternoon, the most delicious smells had been coming out of the kitchen. Aunt Frieda had stayed home from work. When Joey asked why, she'd given him a surprised look and said, "So I can prepare Shabbas dinner, of course," so he'd figured it was one of those Jewish holidays. He only hoped he didn't have to do anything.

Now, Joey was in his room. Bobbie had told him, with considerable disgust, that they had to dress up for Shabbas dinner. He agreed — it was stupid to have to get dressed up, and he wasn't going to do it.

But then he thought, *Aw, might as well. It can't hurt. And it might get me in better with Zeyde and Aunt Frieda. Probably not. But what the heck.*

He put on his good shirt and pants and brushed his hair, doing his best to tame the unruly curls. He put his sneakers away and switched to his brown school shoes. Aunt Frieda would like that. Maybe Zeyde would, too.

Joey tapped on Bobbie's door. "Come in," she yelled crossly.

She was in a light blue dress with a double row of white and dark blue rickrack around the puffy sleeves and hem. On her feet were white anklets and shiny black party shoes. Even her hair was combed. She looked thoroughly miserable.

Joey couldn't resist. "You look . . . nice."

"Shut up!"

He chuckled. If there was any consolation, it was that Bobbie hated getting dressed up more than he did.

Usually they ate in the kitchen, but tonight the dining-room table was covered with a white tablecloth, and the places set with good dishes – white with a thin gold rim.

Zeyde and Aunt Frieda were there, Zeyde in a neat white shirt and black pants, Aunt Frieda in a pretty pink dress. The two adults looked them over. Joey thought he saw grudging approval in Zeyde's eyes, though his grandfather didn't say anything. "Very nice, Joey," Aunt Frieda said with a smile. A small ripple of pleasure went through him.

Aw, don't get carried away, he told himself.

Joey thought they'd sit down to eat, but instead, they gathered in front of the sideboard. On it sat a pair of golden candlesticks with stubby white candles in them, a honey-brown loaf of braided bread, and a silver goblet, encrusted with red and blue stones and covered with strange, square-looking writing, full of wine. Aunt Frieda draped a lacy white scarf over her head, lit the two candles, and began to circle her arms as if pulling the smoke toward herself, chanting in a foreign language.

Watching Aunt Frieda, Joey thought he could see Mama too, but the memory was hazy and the words hazier still.

When Aunt Frieda finished, Zeyde broke off a piece of the bread and held it up. "*Baw-ruch a-taw ah-do-noi . . .*" he said, and Bobbie and Aunt Frieda chimed in. Suddenly

Zeyde broke off. He turned to Joey. "What's the matter, you aren't saying the prayer?"

"I . . . I don't know the words."

"Why not?"

"I . . . just don't. Mama didn't . . ." He didn't want to get Mama in trouble again. "I mean, I never learned them. We didn't do this."

Zeyde's eyebrows gathered. "Never lit the candles? Never said the Shabbas prayers?"

"When I was little . . . maybe."

"Never went to *schul*?"

"N-no."

"No observance, no respect, no nothing," Zeyde said disgustedly. "She just turned her back on her faith – and her duty to her son."

"She didn't do anything wrong!"

"It's a disgrace!"

"It wasn't her fault," Joey said hotly. "You think we had money for candlesticks? There wasn't even enough for food half the time, so you can –"

"No money!" For a moment, Zeyde's expression softened.

"Stop blaming Mama –"

The soft look disappeared. "That's enough out of you!"

"– for every little thing."

"I said that's enough!" Zeyde yelled. "Such a way to talk, and on Shabbas yet." He pointed. "Go to your room."

"But Daddy, what about dinner?" Aunt Frieda sounded dismayed.

"He can eat in his room."

Joey didn't wait to be told again. He turned on his heel and left.

Behind him, he heard Zeyde say forlornly, "She used to hold my hand on the way to *schul*. She used to braid the tassels of my *tallis*. . . ."

Taking the steps two at a time, Joey raced upstairs and slammed his door.

Half an hour later, there was a tap on the door. Aunt Frieda came in with a tray, which she set on the dresser. Her eyes were red from crying.

"Oh, Joey," she sighed, sitting beside him on the bed, "you did it again."

"What'd *I* do?"

"Talked back. Raised your voice."

"He started it. Picking on Mama."

"That's no excuse to be rude."

"I'm not letting him say those things about her. It's not fair."

"But you only make it worse when you lose your temper. And then Zeyde gets mad. And then there's a big fight, and . . . and then Shabbas dinner is ruined!"

Joey saw the tears in her eyes. He thought of how she'd slaved in the kitchen all day. He thought of how pretty she'd looked in the white lacy scarf, and the sweet sound of her voice as she'd sung the prayer.

A pang of remorse stabbed him. But there was no way he was apologizing. All she ever did was take Zeyde's side. She never stuck up for him.

Aunt Frieda sighed. "Oh, Joey, if you could only hold your tongue –"

"*My* fault again!"

"I didn't say that. Come here." She leaned across the bed and gathered him into her arms. Joey stiffened, pushed her away. She got up and quickly left the room.

Joey folded his arms across his chest. He wasn't going to feel bad. He didn't need any hugs from her – they didn't mean anything anyway. She'd given him that big warm hug the first day he'd got here, and look what that was worth. She'd been bossing him around with those stupid rules and siding with Zeyde ever since.

Joey eyed the tray. He should refuse to eat. The smell of roasted chicken made his stomach growl. The aroma of something crisp and savory, something spicy and sweet . . .

He was starving. He set the tray on his bed and tucked in.

There was the same bread Zeyde had been saying the prayer over. It was flaky on the outside, soft on the inside, and so tasty it was almost sweet. Roasted chicken, some white meat and a whole leg. Potatoes, crisp on the outside, flaking to buttery softness on the inside. Sliced tomatoes, oozing pearls of juice. He used a second piece of bread to mop the plate clean.

In a little bowl was some kind of fruit thing, peaches and blueberries with a crunchy cinnamon topping. Joey didn't he think he had room for dessert, but he took a deep breath and plunged in. A few minutes later, he was wiping up the last crumbs with his fingertip.

He leaned back against his headboard and sighed happily. If Shabbas meant eating like this every Friday night, he was happy to be a Jew. He couldn't remember ever eating so much – or such a delicious meal.

Instantly he felt guilty. *Mama was a good cook*, he thought hastily. *She was – in the good times.* Her meatloaf had been scrumptious. Her mashed potatoes had been like velvet. And when she made spaghetti sauce, stirring the pot all afternoon, sprinkling in herbs and spices, her best friend, Connie Busto, said it was like real Italian.

But Mama hadn't done much cooking in the bad times. And even when things were going well, she'd never

74

been able to afford anything but the toughest cuts of meat, the bruised apples, the slightly soft potatoes.

Cooking isn't everything. Mama was good at other things. Like . . . like laughing. And dancing. He smiled, remembering how she used to put on one of her favorite records – Glenn Miller's "In the Mood" – and how they'd jitterbug around the living room. . . .

Then the doorbell would ring, and it would be one of her beaus, and off she'd go, promising not to be late, and sometimes she wouldn't come home all night, and in the morning Joey would find her passed out on the couch. . . .

He jerked himself back to reality. That was over. Now he lived here. And here he was, stuck in his room. Within these four walls. In this prison. Again.

The next morning was Saturday. Joey was leaning on his windowsill, wondering what he and Bobbie would do that day, now that he was allowed out of his room. He heard the front door open and close. Zeyde appeared on the front walk, dressed in a suit. He was carrying a book and a small cloth bag.

A moment later, a man and boy came out of a house a few doors away. The man looked to be Zeyde's age, so Joey supposed the boy was his grandson. They greeted Zeyde and walked on with him.

Joey watched until Zeyde was out of sight, then found Bobbie. "Where's Zeyde going?" he asked.

"To *schul*," she answered.

"She used to hold my hand on the way to *schul*," Joey remembered Zeyde saying last night. So Mama used to go. "What do you do there?" he asked.

"Pray. Sing Shabbas songs."

"I thought Shabbas was last night," Joey said, ready to bristle if she told him again how ignorant he was.

But she didn't. Instead, she explained, "It's Friday night and Saturday. That's how Jewish holidays go – from sundown to sundown."

"Oh." Then he added, "I saw another man and boy walking with Zeyde."

"That must have been Mr. Litvak and his grandson, Peter," Bobbie said. "Lots of men like to go with their grandchildren. The zeydes teach them stuff." She giggled. "And show them off."

Not Zeyde, Joey thought. *He doesn't want to show* me *off. He's probably ashamed to be seen with me. Well, what do I care? I wouldn't want to go with him anyway.*

He forced a smile. "So what are we waiting for? Let's go play."

A few days later, when Joey and Bobbie were lying on the living room floor, reading the sports pages – Joey reading about the Yankees, Bobbie, the Dodgers – Aunt Frieda came in. "What are you two doing reading the paper?" she said. "You haven't done your chores yet."

"Aw, Mama," Bobbie began, "not now."

"Yes now. You know chores are to be done first thing."

"Great!" Joey said. "Now, we've got chores on top of rules."

"Yes, sir. If you're part of this household, you've got to chip in. You can start now, by sweeping the walks. Joey, you take the front, and Bobbie, you take the back. And no sweeping the dirt into the street. You sweep it up in the dustpan and empty it into the trash. Now, get moving."

Muttering "slave driver" under his breath, Joey headed outside with a broom.

Sweeping the walks wasn't all. Joey and Bobbie had to dry the dishes and put them away. Joey had to empty the wastebaskets into the kitchen trash so Zeyde could take it out, and Bobbie had to hang fresh towels in the bathrooms on laundry day.

One day, when Joey and Bobbie were playing in the backyard, Aunt Frieda called them in. She marched Joey upstairs. "What's that pile of clean laundry doing on your bed? I gave it to you an hour ago. You put it away right now."

A minute later he heard Aunt Frieda scolding Bobbie in the kitchen. "Are these your dishes from milk and cookies, young lady?"

"Yes, but I was going to get to them later, Mama."

"You know better. Clean them now, Bobbie."

Joey stopped, a clean T-shirt in his hands. At least Aunt Frieda wasn't just picking on him. She was picking on

Bobbie, too. Something she'd said came back to him: "If you're part of this household . . ."

Aunt Frieda was treating him like a regular family member.

That didn't mean she wanted him to stay.

Still, she was hounding him, just like she hounded Bobbie! She wasn't giving up on him.

But could he trust her? She always went along with Zeyde, and Joey knew Zeyde didn't want him.

The next time it was Joey's turn to dry the dishes, Aunt Frieda gave him a dishtowel and told him to get busy. Joey purposely delayed. He went to the bathroom and combed his hair. He filched a cookie and sat at the kitchen table eating it.

Aunt Frieda came in. "What are you doing, Joey? You've got to pull your load around here, you know. Get moving!"

Joey tried to hide a smile, but Aunt Frieda caught it. She smiled back quizzically. "What are you up to, you rascal?" She gave his bottom an affectionate swat. "Joey, I swear you do this on purpose, just to rile me."

Joey quickly turned away. She'd yelled at him! She expected him to pull his load! It was the best talking-to he'd ever had.

8

Joey and Bobbie walked down the street, heading for the vacant lot. The sun beat down on Joey's shoulders and he could already feel a line of sweat trickling down between his shoulder blades. It was a scorcher, but he wouldn't have cared if it was twice as hot. Today the golden bat was perched on his shoulder, and dangling from the end of it was Bobbie's daddy's glove. Bobbie had casually tossed it to him, and he'd just as casually shoved his ratty old one under the bed. The glove felt so good on his hand. Just like the bat felt so good on his shoulder.

Joey pictured himself leaning on the bat while he shot the breeze with the fellas, as if he leaned on brand-new Louisville Sluggers every day . . . holding it high and ready, waiting for the pitch . . . swinging it around straight and true, for a grand-slam home run. . . .

If I get to play this time, he thought, catching himself. *If the two goons aren't there.*

As he and Bobbie got closer, he saw Grossie, Vito, Louie, and Larry. No sign of Eli and Tommy.

Good.

"Hiya, fellas," Bobbie called.

The boys looked up. "Hey, Bobbie. Joey."

"Hiya, fellas," Joey called back. *They remembered my name.*

"Hey, Joey, you all right now?" Vito asked. "Not too banged up?"

"Yeah, fine." *He cared.*

"Whatcha looking at?" Bobbie asked.

Grossie raised his head. "Did you hear? About Jackie?"

"No, what?" Bobbie asked in alarm. "Is he hurt?"

Louie thrust a newspaper clipping at her. Joey looked over her shoulder. A bizarre sight met his eyes. There was a photo of Jackie Robinson at the plate, and something black on the field near the home team's dugout. The headline said: "Robinson Taunted with Black Cat."

Joey looked closer. Was that what the black smudge was – a cat?

"What!" Bobbie said. "Who did that?"

"The Phillies," Grossie answered.

"The players were ragging him all game. Then they threw a black cat on the field," Larry added. "Then they yelled, 'Hey, Jackie, there's your cousin.' Says here the Philly fans were laughing and cheering."

"But not all of 'em, Lar. Some booed," his twin said.

"Those rats!" Bobbie said. "Those stinking dirty low-down rotten rats!"

"Poor Jackie," Grossie said. "I don't know how he stands it."

Joey felt the heat rush to his face. Everyone knew that Jackie Robinson had faced terrible abuse ever since he'd come up to the majors: name-calling, petitions to keep him off the team, even death threats. And he couldn't fight back, because he'd promised the Dodgers' owner, Branch Rickey, that he wouldn't.

Joey knew how it felt – just like Jackie Robinson did. How people picked on you just because of your color, when you knew that your color had nothing to do with whether you were good or bad. Joey wished he'd been there, in Philadelphia. Maybe Robinson couldn't fight back, but *he* sure could. He'd show those cowards –

Joey caught himself. What the heck was he doing, getting all wound up about Jackie Robinson? Robinson was a Brooklyn player. A Dodger!

Finally, Louie shoved the clipping in his back pocket and they started to play. Bobbie and Vito were named captains, and the kids divided into two sides, Joey, Bobbie, and Grossie against Vito, Larry, and Louie. Because there were only six of them, they decided to play half the field. That meant that, depending on whether a kid batted righty or lefty, only first and second base, or second and third, were in play. There was no catcher, and a throw to the pitcher on the mound, or a forced play, was an out. Joey knew the rules all too well. There'd been plenty of times when he'd only been able to scrounge up a handful of boys – other mixed-race kids who'd been excluded from the Negro kids' teams.

Everyone went to the side of the lot, where a sheet of plywood, with a strike zone marked on it, leaned against the factory fence. They dragged it back and propped it upright behind home plate, anchoring it with big rocks, front and back.

Bobbie and Vito chose for home and away. Vito's team won home first and ran out to the field, Vito on the mound, Larry at shortstop, and Louie in left field. Bobbie, a righty, picked up the bat and stood in the "batter's box," a square outlined in the dirt.

"No batter, no batter," Louie chanted.

"Comin' right atcha, Louie." Bobbie grinned.

Vito threw. Bobbie swung. *Crack!* The ball shot past Larry's outstretched glove and dropped in front of Louie.

Wow, Joey thought, *she can hit*. Bobbie streaked toward first. *Fast, too.*

Louie snatched the ball. Bobbie started sliding as Larry ran to cover Louie's throw. He made the catch, but in a spray of dirt, Bobbie had already tagged.

She jumped up, brushing off her legs and shorts. "Safe!"

"Lucky drop," Vito teased.

"Lucky, my eye," Joey said loyally, and Vito laughed.

Grossie walked to home plate.

"Come on, Grossie, big hit now, you can do it," Bobbie called.

Grossie made wide circles over his shoulder with his bat as if trying to present a moving target.

Vito threw. Grossie swung and missed by half a foot.

"Stee-rike one!" Vito yelled.

"'S'okay, Grossie, you'll get the next one," Bobbie called.

Grossie's bat circled. Vito delivered. *Crack!* A grounder toward third base. "Foul," Vito yelled.

"O and two," Larry said happily. "We got him, fellas."

On the next pitch, his eyes squinting in concentration, his tongue sticking out of the corner of his mouth, Grossie connected. As the ball soared high into near right, he chugged toward first. Looking up, Larry stuck out his glove – and missed.

Bobbie rounded second and sprinted for third. Grossie advanced toward first. Larry ran down the ball and tossed it to Vito – not in time.

"I made it!" Grossie panted. "I got on base!"

"Way to go, Grossie," Joey cheered.

"Okay, Joey, baby, bring us home," Bobbie called from third.

Joey dug his front foot in and raised the bat high over his shoulder. The Louisville Slugger felt smooth and solid in his hands.

The first pitch came in. Joey swung, and even as he came around, he knew it was a good one. The ball hit the "sweet spot" with a satisfying *crack* and then sailed far and high, over Vito's head, over Louie's outstretched glove, heading toward the maple tree.

"Holy cow," Grossie said, standing dumbstruck on first, watching the arc of the ball, as Bobbie raced for home.

"Move, Grossie!" Joey shouted, and with a jolt the redhead lumbered to second.

Louie chased the ball as Bobbie touched home. Grossie chugged, arms pumping. Joey touched first. Grossie rounded second with Joey close on his heels. Louie scooped up the ball.

"Run, Grossie!" Joey yelled. Plodding along, Grossie touched third, with Joey right behind him. Louie threw as

Grossie crossed home. Joey was next, practically treading on Grossie's heels, a split second before the ball landed in Vito's glove.

"Safe!" Bobbie yelled.

"Three runs score!" Grossie said.

"Good hit, Joey," Vito said grudgingly, "even if you did get it off me."

Joey laughed.

By the end of the half-inning, Joey's team had scored five runs, and they were jubilant as they took the field, Bobbie at the mound, Grossie at short, and Joey in the outfield. In short order, Vito and Larry were out. Then Louie came up.

Louie's skinny, Joey thought. *Doesn't look like much of a hitter. Might as well play him in close.*

Crack! A high fly soared back . . . back . . . Cripes! Joey backed up, farther . . . farther . . .

"Watch out!" Bobbie warned.

Then Joey remembered – the maple tree. Too late. His heel caught a root just as the ball fell into his glove. He fell backwards, somersaulted, sprang up – and held up the ball.

"He's got it! What a catch!" Bobbie yelled.

"Sheesh," Louie said forlornly.

Beaming, Joey ran in. Bobbie and Grossie slapped him on the back. This was great – playing ball with friends, teasing and trading insults, falling in the dirt, sweating and cheering, being part of a team. . . .

Joey was just coming up to bat in the second inning when someone roared, "You again?"

He turned. Eli Fishkin. And Tommy Flanagan.

"Shoot," Bobbie muttered. "There goes the game."

Eli pointed at Joey. "I thought I told you you couldn't play here." He jerked his thumb. "Get lost."

Joey looked at the arrogant expression on Eli's face. "Who died and made you king?"

Vito chuckled. "Yeah, I don't remember anybody crowning you, Fishkin."

"Hey, it's King Fish." Joey bulged out his eyes and opened and closed his mouth like a fish.

More chuckles.

"That's not funny," Eli said.

Tommy took a step closer to his friend. "Why's he making like a fish, Eli?" he whispered.

"Shut up, Flanagan," Eli muttered.

"And this one's like an ox – big, dumb Prince Ox," Joey added, pointing at Tommy.

"I am not an ox!" Tommy said. Then, to Eli, "What's an ox?"

"It's like a cow, dummy."

Tommy's ears turned red. "I am not an ox. Or a cow."

The other kids burst out laughing.

Eli gave Joey a shove. "Shut up, Nigger."

"You shut up," Joey returned. "I don't see any crown on your head. You only think there's one."

The other kids murmured agreement.

"Or a throne," Joey added. "Or a – what do you call that thing – you know, that long thing that kings hold?"

"A scepter," Grossie said.

"Right." Joey flashed his friend a smile. "Or a scepter. So I guess you're not king after all."

"Shut up!" Eli's hands balled into fists. His ears turned red. He made as if to go after one kid, then another, but stopped in frustration.

Boy, it's great to be dishing it out for a change, Joey thought. "So, guess what – you don't own the field," Joey said. "We all get to say what goes on here."

"Yeah, Eli!" Louie shouted.

"Eli," Tommy said uneasily, "what's going on? Aren't you going to make him stop?"

"Yeah. Right now," Eli growled. He advanced on Joey until they were practically nose to nose. There was sweat on his forehead. "Shut up!" he blustered. "I *am* in charge. *I* make the rules. *I* say who plays here. And no two-bit punk – especially one who's a nigger – is going to tell me what to do. So scram!"

Joey stood his ground. "Nope."

Eli charged him. Before Joey knew it, he was flat on his back with the other boy on top of him, rocks digging into his spine, Eli's knee pressing into his stomach, and hands squeezing his neck. Joey kicked and twisted from side to side, grinding into the dirt, but couldn't dislodge Eli.

"Quit it, Eli!" Bobbie yelled. "You're choking him!" She grabbed hold of one of Eli's arms with both hands and tugged, and Joey felt a slight lightening of the pressure. Although he was relieved, he wanted to tell her to stay out of it – but before he could get a word out, Tommy had shoved Bobbie and sent her sprawling.

"You big bully," Vito shouted as he entered the fray, "leave her alone!"

Taking advantage of the distraction, Joey managed to roll over and get to his knees, gasping for air. He was grateful that Vito had jumped in to help Bobbie. Maybe together they had a chance of beating Tommy. He struck out again at Eli and a dust cloud rose as the five went at it with surprising fury.

Though it was now three against two, Joey, Bobbie, and Vito were getting creamed. It was clear that the two bigger boys were not just angry, they were enraged.

A bruised and bloodied Vito called to the kids on the sidelines. "Come on, guys! You gonna just stand there?"

Grossie, Larry, and Louie stood in a cluster, looking frightened. Louie made a slight move as if to jump in, but checked himself and stayed where he was.

Bee-e-e-e-p! A loud whistle blasted from the soap factory on the other side of the fence. Moments later, workers started pouring out of the gates in twos and threes, swinging lunch pails, pulling on caps, calling good-byes.

Everyone froze. Eli darted a look over his shoulder and scowled. "Shoot," he said to Tommy. "We'll catch it if they see us fighting. Come on." They scooped up their caps and gloves.

Eli pointed at Joey. "This isn't over. You're gonna learn who calls the shots here."

"Never."

Eli sneered. "I'll finish you off next time." As the first wave of factory workers approached, he and Tommy took off down the street.

Joey turned and surveyed his pals. They looked like they'd been in a prize fight.

Bobbie swiped an arm across her face. "Boy, they were mean today."

"Didn't like getting laughed at," Grossie said. "That's what set 'em off."

"You really had 'em going there, Joey," Larry said.

Joey rolled his eyes. "Fat lot of good it did. We still got pummeled."

"Slaughtered," Bobbie said disgustedly.

Joey turned to Vito. This was the second kid who'd stood up for him. "Thanks, buddy."

"Yeah, thanks, Vito," Bobbie said.

"That's okay," Vito said, shuffling his feet. "Just wish I could have made more of a difference."

"Hey, you were the only reason we didn't get killed," Joey said.

There was a moment of silence.

"Uh . . . sorry, you guys," Louie said in a low voice. "You know . . . for not coming in."

"That's all right," Joey said.

"No. We should've," Larry said sheepishly.

"We were chicken, just plain chicken," Grossie admitted, turning red. "At least, I was."

Louie and Larry nodded, looking uncomfortable.

"Don't worry about it, fellas. It wasn't your fight," Joey said. He sighed. It was his fight, all right, and it looked like he'd have to keep on fighting it – and keep getting pounded – until Fishkin and Flanagan got it through their thick heads that he wasn't going anywhere.

They all retrieved their bats and gloves and said goodbye. Vito, Louie, and Larry went in one direction, Joey, Bobbie, and Grossie in the other.

Bobbie sighed. "We're in for it now," she said.

"I know," Joey said.

"What do you mean?" Grossie asked.

"Zeyde's gonna kill us."

"What for?"

"Fighting," Joey answered.

"But they started it. Eli jumped on you!"

"Doesn't matter."

"But it wasn't your fault! Tell your grandpa that."

"He won't care. He'll still think it's my fault."

They trudged on. Suddenly Grossie stopped. "Wait – I know! Why don't you guys come to my house first? You can wash up there. You get all cleaned up, I bet your grandpa'll never know."

"But Grossie, your mama'll see us, and she'll tell my mama, and –"

"No. She's not home. She's helping out in the store today. And my sister's out, too. Went to see the new Fred Astaire movie with her girlfriends."

Bobbie turned to Joey. "Well? What do you think?"

"He'll know," he said glumly.

"Come on, you guys," Grossie said. Then, earnestly, "It's the least I can do."

Joey thought of Zeyde's wrath. He shrugged. "It's worth a try."

By the time Joey and Bobbie emerged from Grossie's bathroom, two muddy-gray washcloths in hand, scabs were beginning to form on their scrapes and the blood-stains on their clothes were a dull brown.

Grossie surveyed them critically. "Not bad. But you both have bruises on your faces."

Joey shrugged. "Oh, well, nice try."

"Wait!" Grossie cried. "I got another idea. Stay right there." He ran down the hall and came back a moment later with a small compact in his hand.

"What's that?" Bobbie said.

"My sister's face powder."

"Her *what*?"

"Face powder. It'll cover up the marks."

"There's no way you're putting that stuff on me!" Bobbie cried, backing away.

"Or me!" Joey said.

"But you've got to hide those bruises somehow," Grossie argued. "Come on, Joey, at least let me try."

"But makeup's for girls."

"Not *all* girls," Bobbie growled.

"You'd rather get punished?" Grossie said.

Joey thought of Zeyde. If he was caught fighting again . . . would Zeyde really do it? All of a sudden, a little makeup didn't sound so bad. "All right. But just a bit, Grossie."

"Promise," Grossie said. "Close your eyes and hold still."

Something soft and velvety brushed against Joey's forehead. It actually felt nice, though the bruise smarted. Back and forth went the soft pad, light as a feather on his skin.

"There," Grossie said in a satisfied tone. "See, Bobbie? It's almost invisible."

Bobbie peered at Joey. Her expression changed. "Well . . ."

"Told you. Now, hold still." As he approached with the pad, Bobbie squirmed.

Now that he'd gone through it, Joey could enjoy Bobbie's misery. "Oh, dah-ling," he crooned.

"Shut up," she said through gritted teeth.

Joey chuckled. "I think you hate this more than I did, Bobbie."

"I do," she snapped. "I hate girly stuff."

"But you look so glamorous . . ." Joey teased.

She lunged. "I'll give you one!"

"Hold still!" Grossie said. He managed to get the powder on, then led them to the bathroom mirror.

"I got to hand it to you, Grossie," Bobbie said grudgingly. "It works. But the minute we get by Zeyde –"

"*If* we get by Zeyde –"

"– I'm washing it off!"

Joey and Bobbie walked quietly into the house. Zeyde was in his chair in the living room, reading the paper. He looked up. Joey held his breath. Bobbie went very still.

"Been playing ball?" Zeyde asked.

"Yup," Bobbie said, staying in the doorway.

"Have fun?"

"Yup. Sure did. Didn't we, Joey?"

"Uh . . . yeah. Lots of fun."

"You're filthy," Zeyde said.

"That's because . . . we were practicing sliding," Bobbie said. "So we can get good at it. And steal bases. Like Jackie Robinson. Right, Joey?"

"Right."

"And we kept practicing, all afternoon. Leg slides. Stomach slides. So naturally we got dirty and a little banged up. Right, Joey?"

"Right." He elbowed his cousin. She was trying so hard, he was sure she'd tip Zeyde off.

Zeyde gave them an odd look. "I don't mind. It's just dirt." He returned to his paper.

Joey and Bobbie took the steps two at a time, Joey choking down the laughter. He turned to his cousin to congratulate her. But she wasn't there. She was already in the bathroom, washing her face.

A streetcar rumbled down the middle of Utica Avenue, people swaying to and fro as they clung to the overhead straps. A shiny black Studebaker pulled up behind an old white Ford, and the mustachioed driver in a Panama hat beeped his horn importantly, *bee-beep!* A group of old men wearing little round caps sat on a bench, arguing in a strange, throaty language. Three teenage boys strode by, talking baseball.

Across the street, the curved chrome front of Max's Diner gleamed in the sunshine, and the smell of grease and potatoes floated on the air. SUMMER SALE, said a sign in the window of Grossman's Children's Wear. The neon-lit marquee of the Rialto Movie Palace proclaimed THIS SUMMER'S HIT — LORETTA YOUNG & JOSEPH COTTON IN THE FARMER'S DAUGHTER.

Walking down the street between Bobbie and Zeyde, Joey drank it all in. He hadn't been downtown since the day he'd first come to Brooklyn, and even though they were only doing errands today, he wanted to see the sights, smell the smells, meet the people, get to know his new neighborhood.

First stop was Cohen's Bakery. Joey's mouth watered as he looked at the jelly doughnuts sprinkled with sugar, the chunky peanut butter cookies, the cinnamon rolls with plump raisins peeking out like shy children. There was a tray of oatmeal cookies at the side of the store. Joey glanced from left to right, seeing if anyone was looking, and reached his hand out. But his hand stopped in mid-air as he realized he didn't need to steal. There was plenty at home. Strangely, he felt relieved.

While Zeyde picked out a dark brown pumpernickel studded with caraway seeds, a man with a kind-looking plump face and wearing a white apron came out from behind the counter and shook his hand. "How are you, Sam?"

"All right, Irving, how are you?"

"Can't complain. Though I do anyway." He laughed and his stomach shook. He turned to Bobbie. "Hello, Roberta."

"Hi, Mr. Cohen."

He smiled at Joey. "And who's this?"

"My cousin, Joey."

The man looked puzzled for a moment, then nodded. "Oh, you must be Rebecca's boy." He put his hand on Zeyde's shoulder. "I'm so sorry, Sam. I just heard the other day. A terrible loss."

Zeyde stiffened. It wasn't anything you could see, but Joey could feel it. "Thank you, Irving," he said curtly.

"And are you living with your grandpa now?" Mr. Cohen said kindly to Joey.

Joey nodded.

"That's good." He smiled at Zeyde. "A blessing to have another grandchild in the house, eh, Sam?"

For a long moment Zeyde didn't answer. Then he inclined his head. It wasn't a *yes* and it wasn't a *no*.

Joey's heart sank. But what, he asked himself, pushing away a sudden slash of disappointment, had he expected?

Next stop was Stein's Hardware. A tall, balding, dour-looking man with a beaky nose and sunken cheeks said a gloomy hello to Zeyde. He was wearing a canvas apron with many pockets, a ruler poking up from one, a tape measure bulging in another, and a hammer dangling from a loop on the side. He weighed out a bag of nails for Zeyde, took Zeyde's money, and handed Zeyde the bag, all without smiling or saying a word to Bobbie or Joey.

As they were leaving, Joey heard the man say in a low voice to a customer, "So *that's* the boy."

"How can Sam parade him around?" the customer whispered.

"Doesn't look too happy about it," Mr. Stein replied.

"Well, honestly, can you blame him?"

Zeyde was already out the door, so Joey couldn't tell whether he'd heard. He longed to turn around and yell at the men, but forced himself to keep walking.

"Don't pay any mind, Joey," Bobbie whispered. "Mr. Stein's an old meanie. He's miserable to everybody." She gave him a smile, but Joey knew it was one of those smiles that was trying too hard. He didn't smile back.

Then they went to Kaplan's Produce. Mr. Kaplan, a bear of a man with thick, curly black hair, asked Bobbie who her friend was. When she told him, he said, "Pleased to meet you, Joey," and shook his hand as if it were the most natural thing in the world. Then, while Zeyde picked out salad greens, Mr. Kaplan winked at Bobbie and Joey and slipped them each a fat, juicy peach. Joey rubbed the fuzz on his shorts and bit in. Juice dripped down his chin and neck, tickling and feeling sticky at the same time. Licking the nectar off his fingers, he forgot all about Zeyde's stiffness and Mr. Stein's rudeness, the whispers and raised eyebrows.

They turned the corner and entered a large store with a green-and-white striped awning. YANOFSKY'S DELI spelled gold letters on the window. Joey breathed deeply. Tangy pickles . . . sauerkraut . . . smoked herring . . .

Then he remembered. It was in one of Mama's good times, when she'd had some money, and they'd splurged by going out to lunch at a deli on Bergen Avenue. Joey couldn't remember the name of the deli, but he remembered the sandwich. Layer on layer of smoky pastrami between thick slices of rye bread, with spicy mustard and juicy tomato and lettuce. The sandwich was so fat he'd had to stretch his jaw to get his mouth around it, and Mama said he looked like a crocodile eating a big fat toad. He'd finished every bite. And then he'd eaten five whole pickles, one after the other, and he and Mama had laughed all the way home.

He turned to Bobbie. "Did I ever tell you about the time I ate five pickles? At once?"

"You're pulling my leg."

"Am not. Five whole ones. And they weren't weasly ones, either. Great big ones. Mama and I were –"

"Who's the boy, Sam?"

A woman was at the cash register. A plump woman with bulging cheeks, pencilled black eyebrows beneath steel-gray hair, and a red mouth whose color extended beyond the edge of her lips.

A short silence. "My grandson, Joseph."

"Grandson? What grandson? Oh! You mean Rebecca's bas —" She gave a sly smile. "I mean, Rebecca's child?"

"Yes."

"So what's he doing here, Sam?"

Another silence. "Rebecca died."

"She did? How did she die? What happened? Tell me."

A pause. "She just died." Zeyde turned away and started putting things in a basket he carried over his arm.

The woman stared at Joey. Not kindly, like Mr. Cohen and Mr. Kaplan. Coldly, like Mr. Stein. Sizing him up.

She leaned across the counter toward a customer who was unloading her purchases. "You know about Rebecca Greenberg, don't you, Ceil?" she said in a loud whisper. "How she ran away and married a *schvartze*? *If* they were married at all."

Joey turned to Bobbie. "What's that?" he whispered.

"Wh-what?"

"Don't pretend you didn't hear."

She turned red. "Never mind."

"Oh no, you don't. Tell me."

She hesitated. "It's Yiddish. Means black."

A beat. Then it sank in. "Nigger."

Bobbie nodded.

". . . such a scandal, I tell you, Ceil," the woman said, punching the cash register keys. "After all, this is a respectable neighborhood. Or it *was*, anyway, until *she* started carrying on . . ."

Joey glanced at Zeyde. Although his grandfather's back was turned toward the woman and he was busy choosing a can of coffee from the shelf, Joey knew that this time he'd heard. He had to have heard, the way her voice shrilled across the store. Zeyde's face was hard and cold, the way it got when he was angry. Joey knew that look well, and for once he was glad to see it. Any minute now, Zeyde would give that lady what-for and that would shut her up.

But Zeyde said nothing.

". . . no good to begin with, so what do you expect?" the woman was saying. The customer nodded in agreement.

Say something, Zeyde, Joey thought. *You're not going to let her get away with it, are you?*

His jaw clenched, Zeyde put a can of sardines in his basket and moved down the row.

". . . a wild girl, and then to live in sin like that. Well, I tell you . . ."

Joey glanced at Bobbie. She too was looking at Zeyde as if willing him to speak up.

Please, Zeyde, Joey thought desperately. *I know you're mad at Mama. And at me. But you can't let her go on like this!*

Zeyde took a bottle of ketchup off a high shelf. His face was purple. *He must be furious with the woman,* Joey thought. *So why doesn't he do anything?*

". . . never to be heard from again. And then for the brat to just turn up like that. Well! Did you ever?"

Joey's ears were hot. He felt like grabbing the lady by the collar and telling her to shut up her fat face. But he knew he mustn't. He'd been in enough trouble already. And if he did . . .

But why didn't Zeyde do it?

". . . well, filth breeds filth, that's what I always say. . . ."

Filth!

Joey cast one last look at Zeyde. Not a whisper of protest. Not a flicker of outrage.

He marched over and slapped his hands on the counter. "Shut up!"

The woman looked up, startled, her mouth a round, red *O*.

"Don't you say those things about me and my mama!"

Bobbie chimed in, "Yeah, Mrs. Yanofsky!"

"Why, you little —"

"And I'm not a sh — shvar — whatever you said —"

"How dare you!"

"And my mama was not filth —"

"Of all the disgraceful —"

"And neither am I!"

"You tell her, Joey!" Bobbie said.

The woman looked triumphantly at her customer. "It just goes to show –"

"You don't know anything, so stop telling lies, you mean old –"

"Silence!"

"– rotten liar!"

"SILENCE!"

A hand gripped his shoulder. Fingers bit in.

Zeyde threw his basket onto the counter and, without releasing his hold on Joey, marched him out of the store. Bobbie trailed behind. A wave of murmurs followed them.

Outside, Zeyde gripped Joey's shoulders with both hands and shook him. His black eyes seemed to bore holes in Joey's. "You troublemaker! Don't you *ever* speak that way again!"

"But she said –"

"I don't care what she said."

"But Zeyde," Bobbie cut in, "you heard her –"

"That's enough, Bobbie."

"No one's going to talk about Mama like that!" Joey shouted.

Zeyde turned back to him. For a moment, less than a moment, his expression changed, and Joey thought maybe Zeyde was proud of him. But then Zeyde scowled even more darkly. "It's not for you to say, you little hellion! She's your elder, and you don't raise your voice to your elders."

"But —"

"No buts, you hear me? Not another word!" He shook Joey again. "You've shamed me. Shamed me in my own neighborhood." He released Joey, practically flinging him away, turned, and started walking home.

Joey stood, watching his grandfather walk away from him. And he faced the truth. There was only one reason Zeyde hadn't told the woman off — because he agreed with her. Because he believed that Mama was a disgrace. Because he was ashamed of his half-breed grandson.

Joey's eyes pricked.

Don't you dare cry! What did you expect? And who cares anyway?

His eyes brimmed as he blindly trudged home.

Aunt Frieda was sniffling. Stuck in his room — with the door open a crack — Joey could hear her. "Oh, dear, such an embarrassment."

"Embarrassment doesn't begin to describe it," Zeyde snapped. "It was a disgrace."

Then, footsteps on the stairs. "But Zeyde, you didn't tell her —" Bobbie's voice.

"What are you doing here, Bobbie?" Zeyde said sharply. "This is between your mama and me."

"But you didn't tell Mama what Mrs. Yanofsky said," Bobbie insisted. "She called him a *schvartze*, Mama —"

"What!"

"Bobbie, leave us alone," Zeyde said.

"Is that true, Daddy?"

"It makes no difference. The mouth on him —"

"And all kinds of bad things about his mama —"

"About Becky?" Aunt Frieda sounded shocked.

"Bobbie, that's enough!"

"And how they were no good and Joey was filth —"

"*What?*"

"Bobbie! Leave us now!"

There was a short silence as Bobbie left the room. But Joey didn't hear her feet on the stairs, so he figured she must be hiding in the hallway.

"Is that true, Daddy?" Aunt Frieda said in a sharper tone.

"Yes, but —"

"No wonder he was upset! That poor boy, to stand there and —"

"Poor boy!"

Aunt Frieda paused. "I think . . . that is . . . you should have stuck up for him, Daddy," she said.

"Frieda!"

"Well . . . how could you let her say those things?"

"What, I should let my grandson insult a respectable storekeeper, in front of everybody?"

"Respectable! Sadie Yanofsky is the biggest *yenta* in Brooklyn and everybody knows it."

"Frieda!"

Joey heard a stifled giggle. Bobbie. He wondered what a *yenta* was.

"Well, it's true," Aunt Frieda said. "Filth! Did she really say that?"

Zeyde grunted.

"Oh, Daddy, how could you just stand there? How could you not shut her up?"

"What, and dignify the ravings of the likes of Sadie Yanofsky? Besides," Zeyde's voice rose, "the point isn't what *I* did or didn't do, it's what *he* did. It was outrageous. He's getting worse, Frieda. You know he is."

"Maybe we're going about it the wrong way, Daddy. Maybe we're handling him wrong."

"What! You don't think he needs to be brought into line?"

"I do . . . but all this punishing and yelling doesn't seem to be helping."

"He'd be ten times worse without it! It's like Becky all over again. I was too lax with her, but I won't be with him. Though who knows if anything will work with that boy?" He paused. "Maybe he should go back, Frieda."

"Daddy!"

Joey froze.

Zeyde's voice changed, and he was nearly crying. "Frieda, we're failing! And if we can't succeed –"

"No, Daddy! We're not failing. We're not going to. And Joey is not Becky. He's a fine boy. Please, have a little more patience."

"I can't fail!" It seemed to be torn out of him.

"No, of course not, Daddy. We'll bring him around."

There was a long silence. "If only I could believe that."

"*I* believe it," Aunt Frieda said.

Joey quickly shut his door. He was safe – for a little while longer.

Not that he cared one way or the other.

Oh, stuff it, he thought. That wasn't working anymore, because the truth was, he wanted to stay. He couldn't deny it any longer; couldn't pretend he didn't care.

I believe it, Aunt Frieda had said. It warmed Joey just to remember the words.

But Zeyde –

Wait a minute. *Ravings.* Zeyde had said, *The ravings of the likes of Sadie Yanofsky.* Joey rolled that around in his head, trying to figure out what it meant. Could it be that Zeyde thought Mrs. Yanofsky was wrong, too?

Oh, if only Joey could believe *that*.

CHAPTER

10

H ours later, Joey leaned out of his window, resting his elbows on the sill, trying to catch a breeze. He'd been grounded for the rest of the afternoon and all through dinner. He'd eaten another meal alone, from a tray.

The air was still and heavy. Joey fanned his face with his hand. No relief. He leaned out farther. The old woman who lived across the street rocked on her stoop, back and forth, back and forth. A man walked by, his shirt a flag of white in the gathering dusk, his footsteps tapping an even beat. A fragrance of roses drifted up from the neighbor's garden, the smell of someone's fish dinner. Joey listened to the evening sounds: mothers calling their kids, crickets singing, the distant rumble of the streetcar. A horn honked, a screen door clicked shut.

Bored, bored, bored. Joey examined his Yankees collection. His team had won again, and he'd added a new clipping, a picture of Snuffy Stirnweiss clouting a home run, the ball a small white blur in the distance, Snuffy looking up with a smile on his face. Joey moved the picture an inch to the left. Straightened his Joe DiMaggio card.

He paced. Ten steps to the door. Ten steps back. Ten steps to the door. Ten steps back.

Downstairs, the radio shut off. Footsteps on the stairs. The sound of a toilet flushing. The house grew quiet.

Joey changed into pajamas. He lay on his bed, hands beneath his head. There was no way he was going to be able to fall asleep. It was all Zeyde's fault. If his grandfather had only stuck up for him with that woman, he wouldn't have got into trouble. And then he wouldn't have been grounded. Then he wouldn't be so restless.

He sat up. What was he doing in here? There was no way he was staying in this room one more minute, and if his grandfather thought he could make him, he had another think coming. Getting sent to his room never used to keep him in. Why, he'd snuck along the ledge from the bathroom window to the fire escape outside Mama's apartment so many times that his footprints were practically etched into the stone.

So why not here? He could sneak out and sneak back in before anyone knew. Get a breath of fresh air, stretch his legs, see the stars. And besides, he'd get back at Zeyde.

Joey tiptoed to the door. All quiet. But what if the stairs squeaked? No, better not risk it. He turned and eyed the window. A better bet. He eased the sash up higher and squeezed out onto the roof. It sloped gently toward the street. Not too steep. He'd been on worse. He squatted there. All quiet. Dark. Good. He crept over the peak, around to the back of the house. Carefully he sat down and dangled his feet over the roof ledge. This was more like it. The damp green smell of grass filled the air. It was still hot, but there was a slight breeze out here, enough to stir the sleeves of Joey's pajama top. Better than in his room. His prison cell. Might as well have bars on the windows.

Bars. Suddenly Joey remembered seeing bars on the back of the house. A fire escape! Not the kind with spiraling stairs, like at Mama's, but a sort of ladder with iron rungs, built into the back wall. Why, he wasn't stuck up here! He could climb down, take a stroll around the block, maybe even scoot over to Utica Avenue and see what was happening. He was free!

Because of the roof's overhang, he couldn't see the top rung. But he was pretty sure that if he turned over onto his stomach and felt with his foot, he'd be able to locate it.

Just as he was about to flip over, he heard the sound of a match striking, smelled sulphur and then, a moment later, cigarette smoke. He looked from side to side. There was no red glow of a cigarette tip in the backyard of the Shapiros' house to the left, or in the Nussbaums' yard to the right. *Must have come from someone's kitchen window, then.*

Carefully Joey turned over onto his stomach. There was nothing for his hands to grab onto, so, keeping his weight on his chest, he groped with his foot. Where was the bar? There. He put his weight on it, then, clinging to the roof with his upper body, slid down a little farther, feeling with his other foot. A pebble came loose from the roof and pinged off the back kitchen railing. Motionless, Joey held his breath. Nothing. *Whew.* He felt the bar and was just stepping onto it when –

"What's that? Who's up there?"

Zeyde!

All Joey saw were the whites of Zeyde's eyes and the glowing tip of his cigarette. Frantically, he tried to heave his leg back up and over the roof ledge.

"Joey! Oh, my God!" Zeyde cried. "You rascal! Of all the – Get down here this minute!"

For a panicky second, Joey thought of climbing back up, scooting back in his window, diving into bed, and pretending it had all been a figment of Zeyde's imagination. But he knew it wouldn't work. Besides, he couldn't reach his leg back up to the ledge. Reluctantly, he started climbing down, rung by rung.

Footsteps pounded down the stairs, out the kitchen door.

"Daddy, what's going on? Is it an intruder?"

"Oh, I hope so!" Bobbie squealed.

Joey climbed down the last few bars. As soon as he dropped onto the grass, Zeyde grabbed him by the arm, whether to keep him from harm or keep him prisoner, Joey couldn't tell.

"Joey!" Even in the dim light he could see the shock in Aunt Frieda's eyes. She looked up at the roof. "Did he –?"

"Holy Toledo!" Bobbie said. At least someone was impressed.

"Go back to bed, you two. I'll deal with this."

"But Daddy, he might be hurt –"

"He's fine."

"But what if –"

"I said go back to bed."

Meekly, Aunt Frieda and Bobbie went inside. Bobbie gave him a light punch as she went by to wish him luck.

He'd need it. He'd really done it now. His stomach clenched as Zeyde's words came back to him: *Maybe he should go back.*

Zeyde pulled him up the steps, squeezing his arm.

"Ow! You're hurting me!"

"You'll hurt more when I'm through with you."

So he was going to get spanked. Well, that was nothing new; he'd been spanked before. Only, Mama had never put her heart in it. Somehow he had a feeling that Zeyde would. Still, spanking was better than –

Zeyde dragged Joey across the kitchen, down the hall, up the stairs, and threw him onto his bed. He glanced at the open window, then back at Joey, a thunderous look on his face. "Where did you think you were going?"

"Just . . . out."

"Just like that?"

Joey shrugged. "I used to do it all the time. Mama never knew."

There was a sharp intake of breath. "Climbing out windows? Balancing on roofs?"

"Yeah."

"And if you slipped?" His voice rising.

"What would you care? You'd probably be happy if I broke my neck. Then you'd be rid of me."

Zeyde's face turned red. *'Cause I guessed the truth*, Joey thought with a bitter sense of triumph.

There was a long pause. Then, "Pull down your pants."

Joey obeyed. He wouldn't cry, no matter what. Wouldn't give the old man the satisfaction.

Zeyde turned him over his knee and gave him a sharp smack. It stung. Joey gritted his teeth. Zeyde grunted with each slap. No tears! Another. Another. Finally, Zeyde lifted him, breathing hard. Joey pulled up his pants.

Zeyde grabbed Joey by the shoulders. His eyes bored into Joey's. His voice was low, but intense. "Now, you listen and you listen good. You will stop this wildness. You will do as you're told. You will not sass back. And you will stay in this room all day tomorrow if I have to sit on the roof myself. Do you hear me?"

No answer.

"Answer me!"

"Yes, Zeyde!"

"I'm going to teach you to behave if it's the last thing I do! DO YOU HEAR ME?"

"Yes, Zeyde." Not giving an inch.

Zeyde stared at him for a long moment, his eyes fierce. Then he strode from the room, slamming the door.

Joey sat heavily on his bed. Ouch! His bottom burned. Tears sprang to his eyes. He would not cry. He wouldn't. He blinked back the tears.

He didn't know why Zeyde hadn't sent him away this time. *Maybe*, Joey thought bitterly, *Zeyde is having too much fun punishing me. Or maybe . . .* Just before, when Zeyde had seen Joey on the roof, he'd cried out, and for just that moment, Joey had thought –

No, forget it. He'd been mistaken.

Carefully he lay down on his side. He took several deep breaths. Hugging his pillow to his chest, he fell asleep.

11

A few days later, Joey was pinning his latest Yankees clipping to his bulletin board – "Reynolds Gets Shutout in Yankees' 5-0 Win Over Chi-Sox" – when there was a knock on the door.

Bobbie stuck her head in. "There's a Dodgers-Cardinals game on the radio. You want to listen with Zeyde and me?"

"Hmm . . ." Joey said. "Didn't the Cardinals win the World Series last year?"

"Yeah. So?"

"Sure. It'll be fun to hear Brooklyn lose."

"We're going to win this one."

"Yeah, sure."

With a *hmmph*, Bobbie slammed the door and pounded down the stairs. Pulling on his Yankees cap, Joey followed her into the living room. Zeyde was in his customary chair by the window, fiddling with the radio dials. Bursts of static alternated with the voice of the Dodgers announcer.

Zeyde turned when Joey came in. Their eyes met. A strange truce had existed between them since the spanking. Joey had been careful not to raise his voice, or disobey, or pull any pranks. He'd done his chores and followed the rules. He hadn't been in any more trouble, and that was a relief.

Yet he felt uneasy, too. Zeyde didn't hug him or ruffle his hair or joke with him, the way he did with Bobbie. He kept his distance. Sometimes Joey felt his grandfather's eyes on him, almost swallowing him. But as soon as Joey turned, Zeyde would look away. It made Joey feel weird. In a crazy way, he almost liked it better when Zeyde was mad at him – at least he knew where he stood.

Zeyde finished tuning the radio, leaving the volume low during the pre-game chatter. Bobbie opened a drawer in the little table, pulled out a blue-and-white Dodgers pennant and draped it over the radio, carefully smoothing it flat. Now Joey saw that, in addition to their blue Brooklyn baseball caps, she and Zeyde were dressed all in blue – pants, shirts, even socks.

Joey laughed. "That ain't gonna help."

"Will so," Bobbie said.

"Wearing blue socks? Putting a banner over the radio? Come on."

"The pennant's gonna bring us a pennant," said Bobbie.

Joey rolled his eyes. "You're more desperate than I thought. How about a rabbit's foot?"

Bobbie gasped. "I almost forgot!" She reached into her pocket, pulled out a ratty-looking gray rabbit's foot on a chain, and laid it on top of the banner.

Joey hooted. "How about a witch doctor? Or a sorcerer?"

To his surprise, Joey saw Zeyde's lips twitch.

"Oh, shush," Bobbie said.

Joey snatched the rabbit's foot and addressed it. "Oh, magic rabbit's foot, cast a spell on the Cardinals and make them lose – after all, how else are we going to win?" Bobbie grabbed for the rabbit's foot but he swung it back and forth, out of reach. "Hocus-pocus alla-docus, abracadabra higgledy-poo . . ."

Bobbie and Zeyde burst out laughing.

He'd made Zeyde laugh!

Bobbie gave Joey a smack. "Cut it out." She grabbed the rabbit's foot and laid it carefully on the pennant. "We do *not* need magic. We won our last game and we're going to make it two in a row. Right, Zeyde?"

His eyebrows furrowed. "I don't know, Bobbele. Last time we faced the Cardinals, they clobbered us."

She patted his knee. "Don't be a worrywart. This is the beginning of a winning streak, you'll see."

The last strains of "The Star Spangled Banner" faded away. Zeyde turned up the volume, then settled back in his chair. Bobbie leaned against his legs. Joey sat in the chair opposite Zeyde's.

Good aftuhnoon, ladies and gentlemen, and welcome to Dodgers baseball, said a high-pitched voice with a strong Southern drawl. *This is Red Barber, live from Ebbets Field, where today the Brooklyn Dodgers take on the world champion St. Louis Cardinals. The Cardinals are contenduhs again this yeah, thanks to their talented outfield, led by Enos Slaughter. But Dodgers starter Ralph Branca has been throwing smoke lately, so we should have a dandy contest this afternoon, yessuh.*

"Branca's got the best E.R.A. on the Dodgers," Bobbie said.

"Yeah, but Slaughter pounded him last time," said Zeyde.

Leading off for the St. Louis Cardinals, outfielder Enos Slaughter, Red Barber said, and Bobbie groaned. *Slaughter's hitting an impressive .308. And heah's the first pitch, a curveball, letter-high. Slaughter swings, he misses. Strike one. It's O and one. . . .*

Slaughter connected on the second pitch, hitting a high fly ball, but Dodger outfielder Pete Reiser caught it for the first out.

"Hooray!" Bobbie and Zeyde cheered.

From outside Joey heard an echoing cheer. ". . . ray-ray-ray . . ." It seemed to bounce from living room to living room, all the way down the street. The whole neighborhood was cheering!

The second Cardinals batter made it safely to first on a line drive to right field.

"Uh-oh," Bobbie said.

Whitey Korowski was up next.

Korowski stands in. Branca winds up. It's a curveball. Korowski swings. It's a grounder to left, looks like a hit. . . . But wait, heah's Reese, he's got it on a bounce. Reese fires to Stanky for the out at second. Stanky spins and throws, oh my, it's short, Robinson stretches at first, will he get it? . . . Yes! Ladies and gentlemen, Robinson's got it to make the double play and reti-uh the side.

Another cheer, louder than the last, swept like a wave through the neighborhood.

A discordant clamor of bleeps and bangs came over the radio. At first it just sounded like noise, but then a melody emerged, and a great chorus of fans started singing, *The worms crawl in, the worms crawl out, they eat your guts and they spit them out.*

"What's that racket?" Joey asked.

Bobbie looked at him incredulously. "Ain't you ever heard of the Dodgers Sym-*phony* Band?"

Joey shook his head.

Bobbie grinned. "It's a bunch of fans. They bring drums and bugles to the games. Make music every time we get the other side out."

"You call that music?"

Bobbie dismissed him with a flap of the hand as she and Zeyde joined in. "Your stomach turns a slimy green . . ." Zeyde clapped in rhythm, his face alight. Joey gaped. This sure wasn't the Zeyde he knew.

With a loud screech, the music ended, and the bottom of the first inning was underway.

"Now you'll see our bats talking!" said Bobbie.

In quick order, two Dodgers singled, putting runners on first and second.

Bobbie smiled triumphantly. "What do you say now, mister?"

Leaning back in his chair, Joey folded his arms. "Check with me in nine innings."

The next batter flied out, but Eddie Stanky, the second baseman, walked.

Bases loaded with one out, Barber said. A hush fell over the crowd. *Next up is Bruce Edwards, the catcher. Here's the windup. A fastball. Edwards chops it. Brazle has it, he fires to first, there's one out. Stan Musial throws home. Garagiola, tags, beating the runnuh. It's a double play for the Cardinals to end the inning.*

Bobbie groaned. Zeyde groaned. The crowd groaned. The street groaned.

And at the end of the first inning, no runs, two hits, no erruhs, and the Dodgers leave three runnuhs on base. And now, a word from our sponsor.

"Next inning," Bobbie said. "You'll see."

Joey just smiled.

In the top of the second, the Cardinals scored two runs. Then, leading off for Brooklyn in the bottom of the second, PeeWee Reese doubled, and the street rang with hurrahs.

That brings up the first baseman, Jackie Robinson, Barber said. Amid the cheers came shouts of "Nigger!" followed by booing. *The St. Louis players are riding Robinson something fierce as he makes his way to the plate.*

"Jerks," Bobbie snapped, and Joey silently agreed. Poor Jackie, putting up with all that crap.

Robinson pays no notice. He's all concentration out theah. Brazle goes into his motion. Robinson swings – it's a line drive to center. Reese is on his way to third . . . safe! It's a single for Robinson.

"Yay!" Bobbie and Zeyde cried.

That brings up Gene Hermanski, the third baseman. Runners on first and third. Robinson takes a lead, one step, another. . . . Oh, the crowd's humming, they want Robinson to steal. . . .

Joey found himself leaning forward, along with Zeyde and Bobbie, spurring Robinson on.

Brazle throws a fastball . . . and theah goes Robinson! The catcher's got the ball . . . and heah's the throw – Joey's breath held. *Not in time! Robinson's safe at second and the fans are on their feet. My, oh my, that's the sixteenth stolen base of the season for the talented young rookie!*

A grin creased Joey's face. He wiped it off before Bobbie saw.

Robinson's steal seemed to ignite the Dodgers. In the top of the third, they held the Cardinals scoreless, then scored three runs in their half of the inning. By the top of the sixth, Brooklyn led, four to two.

"What'd I tell you!" Bobbie said.

With the Cardinals trailing, the leadoff batter is Enos Slaughter. He takes the first pitch, low and inside. Ball one . . . Slaughter has been very vocal about his opposition to a Negro being allowed to play in the National League. . . . Heah's Branca's second pitch. Slaughter fouls it back, out of play. . . . He's been baiting Robinson every time he gets near him. Branca delivers a fastball. Slaughter swings, it's a chopper to second. Stanky runs it down, makes the throw to first. Robinson reaches for the ball, Slaughter starts sliding, his foot comes up – oh my, he kicked Robinson! Enos Slaughter has deliberately spiked Jackie Robinson! Robinson's down –

"What!" Bobbie shouted.

What a shameful spectacle. Red Barber sounded distressed. Behind him, the crowd roared in outrage. Joey felt outraged, too. Of all the cowardly, disgusting things! Calling names was bad, and throwing a cat on the field was worse, but purposely hurting another player was *really* low.

Robinson's on his feet. He's obviously in pain. It looks like Slaughter's taunting him, but Robinson, of course, can't do anything, because of his promise to Mr. Rickey. But Robinson is not happy, no suh.

"That snake!" Bobbie said.

But now the boos were turning to cheers. Shouts and hurrahs and applause. *What's this?* Barber said. *Wait a minute – here comes PeeWee Reese. He's walking over to Robinson's side. He's yelling at Enos Slaughter. Here comes Ralph Branca, the pitcher. Here comes Eddie Stanky. Gene Hermanski, over from third. The outfielders. They're all gathering around Robinson. And who's this? . . . Oh my!* Barber sounded amazed. *It's Dixie Walker!*

Joey glanced at Zeyde. There were tears in his grandfather's eyes. Joey knew why. He knew about Dixie Walker – everybody did. How he'd started a petition to try to keep the "nigger" off the team. How, earlier in the season, he'd refused to shake Robinson's hand. And now –

Joey felt all choked up, too. To his surprise, his own eyes filled.

The whole Dodgers dugout has stormed onto the field! They're all standing behind their teammate, Jackie Robinson, Barber said jubilantly.

"Isn't that great, Zeyde?" Bobbie said. Joey quickly wiped his eyes.

"Hey, I saw that."

"What? I got dust in my eyes."

"Yeah, sure. You were blubbering over Robinson."

"I was not blubbering!"

"Were so. Wasn't he, Zeyde?"

Zeyde nodded. "Looked a little choked up to me."

"Aw, get out. What do I care?"

"Bet you're softening up on the Dodgers."

"You're nuts," Joey blustered.

Of course he didn't care about the Dodgers. Or Robinson.

Did he?

Well . . . forget the Dodgers. But heck, a fella couldn't help caring about Jackie Robinson. His incredible speed. His blazing bat. Most of all, the way he held his head high in the face of the constant abuse, and just played his game. Of course Joey admired that.

He sure wasn't going to admit it to Bobbie, though. He'd never hear the end of it!

The game resumed. The Dodgers got three hits in the bottom of the sixth, but were unable to score. In the top of the seventh, Branca walked three in a row, then allowed a triple that tied the game. He was yanked.

"Don't worry, Zeyde, Casey'll save it," Bobbie said as the reliever was brought in.

Casey gave up two quick base hits, then the go-ahead run.

"We'll get it back, Zeyde."

The Dodgers stranded two runners in the seventh.

"Two more innings to go. We'll rally."

Another Cardinals home run.

"Not again," Bobbie wailed. "Please not again."

A Brooklyn error.

Bobbie groaned.

And the final score, St. Louis eight, Brooklyn four, Red Barber said mournfully. Zeyde switched off the radio and an answering stillness enveloped the street as the radios of Brooklyn fell silent.

Bobbie slumped back against Zeyde's legs. He rested his hands on her shoulders. "Well . . ." she said to Joey, "aren't you going to rub it in?"

Joey thought about it. He could say I told you so. He could point out how satisfying it was to root for winners instead of a bunch of bumblers who always broke your heart.

But, looking at Bobbie and Zeyde snuggled together, sharing their misery, he felt a swift pang of . . . what? He didn't know. He just knew he wasn't in the mood for teasing anymore.

"Nah," he said, trying to sound jaunty, "I'll cut you a break – this time."

Tugging down his Yankees cap, he left them huddled together by the radio.

12

The next day, after breakfast, when Aunt Frieda was at work, Zeyde announced that he was going to rearrange the furniture in his room so he could move his bed near the window and catch a breeze at night.

"Okay," Bobbie said absently, and went upstairs.

Joey stayed in the kitchen, reading the sports pages. Soon he heard grunts coming from Zeyde's room. He tiptoed down the hall and peeked in. Zeyde was stripped down to his undershirt. He was heaving against a dresser, but it wasn't going anywhere. Joey watched for a moment. Then he ran upstairs. "Come on," he said to Bobbie, "we've got to help Zeyde."

"What do you two want?" Zeyde asked when they appeared in his doorway. His forehead was beaded with sweat.

"We've come to help," Bobbie said. "It was Joey's idea."

Zeyde looked at Joey with an odd expression for so long that Joey squirmed. "Was it, now?" he finally said.

They stripped Zeyde's bed and threw the sheets on the living-room couch. They pulled out the dresser drawers and stacked them in the hallway, undershirts on top of underpants on top of socks on top of pajamas. That left the bookcase. Loading up with as many books as they could carry, the three of them took turns carrying armloads of books into the living room and stacking them in towers on the floor. Some of the books smelled old, and their pages were yellow. Some had pages that were edged in gold, so that from the side, they looked like small, flat, golden treasure chests.

Emptying the top shelf, Joey picked up a blue velvet bag that zipped at the top and a black book with strange writing on the cover, which Joey supposed must be Hebrew. *These are the things I saw Zeyde carrying to* schul *that day*, he thought. When his grandfather was in the other room, he whispered to Bobbie, "What's in the bag?"

"Zeyde's *tallis*," she answered. "His prayer shawl."

She used to braid the tassels of my tallis . . . Joey remembered Zeyde saying that first Shabbas night. He'd sounded broken-hearted, as if he really missed Mama doing that.

As he carried his armload out of the room, Joey wondered what Zeyde's prayer shawl looked like, and how he prayed in it. *Maybe he'll take me with him to* schul *someday*, he thought.

Finally, when the bookcase was empty, Zeyde took a photograph down from the top. It was of a woman – a nice woman, from the quick look that Joey took. "Who's that?" he said.

"Bubbeh," Bobbie told him.

"Who?"

"My grandma. *Our* grandma," she corrected.

Mama's mother, Joey thought.

Zeyde held out the picture for Joey to see.

She was plump, double-chinned and round-cheeked, with big round eyes. *The same as Mama's and Aunt Frieda's*, Joey thought. Her mouth was turned up in a gentle smile. She looked like the kind of mother you could pour out your troubles to, and she'd give you a kiss and a hug and somehow everything would be better.

"Did you know her?" Joey asked Bobbie.

She shook her head. "She died when Mama – my mama and your mama – were teenagers."

Zeyde didn't say anything. He just gazed at the picture. Joey felt a swift stab of sympathy.

Grunting and heaving, the three of them moved the bed to where the dresser was, the bookcase to where the bed was, and the dresser to where the bookcase was. Then they put all the drawers and books away.

"Look at you!" Joey laughed, pointing at Bobbie. Her cheeks were smudged with dust, and the fronts of her shirt and shorts were brownish-gray.

"You, too," Bobbie said, and they both laughed.

Zeyde wiped his forehead with his arm, leaving a dirty smear on his face. He reached into his pocket, pulled out two nickels and dropped one into each of their hands.

Joey could have kicked himself, but it slipped out before he thought. "You don't have to pay us, Zeyde."

Zeyde shook his head with a smile. "That's all right. A little treat doesn't hurt."

"Thanks!" Joey and Bobbie said together.

Bobbie turned to Joey. "What are you going to spend yours on?"

"Baseball cards," he said without a moment's hesitation.

"Me, too!"

There was a brief discussion with Zeyde, who at first was not inclined to let them go up to Gershon's on Utica Avenue by themselves, but relented after they washed their hands and faces, changed their clothes, and promised that they'd go straight to the store and straight back.

And pick him up a cigar while they were at it.

And not tell Aunt Frieda.

Faces clean, hair combed, clutching the precious nickels, Joey and Bobbie entered Gershon's Drugstore.

Joey remembered being in there with Miss MacNeill on his first day in Brooklyn. How long ago that seemed!

Bobbie led Joey to the front counter, where a woman with short, brown, gray-flecked hair and green eyes stood at the cash register. Behind her, glass shelves held cigarettes, packages of Wrigley's chewing gum, and boxes of red-banded cigars.

"Hi, Mrs. Gershon," Bobbie said.

"Hi, Bobbie. Who's this?"

"My cousin, Joey. Joey, this is Mrs. Gershon."

"Your cousin?" The woman frowned in confusion. Joey tensed. Was she going to be one of the mean ones, like Mr. Stein and Mrs. Yanofsky?

Recognition dawned on the woman's face. Her hand flew to her heart. Tears filled her eyes. "Oh, my God. Becky's boy."

Joey relaxed.

She reached her hand across the counter. "So good to meet you – Joey, is it?"

Joey nodded, sending her a smile. Her clasp was warm and firm.

She wiped her eyes, shaking her head. "Should have known. You look just like her."

"Did you know my mama?" Joey asked.

"Did I know her!" Mrs. Gershon repeated, waving a

hand. "Sure I knew her. Like a little sister. I used to babysit her and Frieda."

"You did?" Joey asked. "What were they like?"

Mrs. Gershon's eyes sparkled. "Devils, that's what. Every time I had to babysit those two, I knew I was in for it. That Becky was always playing jokes."

"Like what?"

"Well . . . one time she put a cricket in my pocketbook, and when I opened it, it jumped out and I nearly had a heart attack."

Bobbie and Joey laughed.

"And she never went to bed when she was supposed to," Mrs. Gershon added. "Popping up every minute, hopping into Frieda's bed, coming downstairs for a drink of water. Boy, was she a live wire!"

Joey nodded.

Mrs. Gershon went on, "One time when I was baby-sitting, Frieda went right to sleep, like she always did. But no matter what I did, I couldn't get Becky to sleep. I read her stories. I rubbed her back. Nothing worked. Finally, I was so worn out, *I* fell asleep! Hours later, when your Bubbeh and Zeyde came home, it was Becky who greeted them at the door, wide awake. 'Hi, Mama, hi, Daddy, did you have a good time?'"

All three of them laughed. *How wonderful to hear happy memories of Mama*, Joey thought.

Bobbie asked to see the baseball cards, and Mrs. Gershon lifted down a cardboard box. Inside were dozens of small packets, each containing a baseball card and a flat rectangle of pink bubble gum. "You a Dodgers fan, Joey?" she asked.

Before he could answer, Bobbie said, "Nah, he's from the Bronx."

Mrs. Gershon gasped. "A Yankees fan! Outa my store."

Startled, Joey looked up. She was smiling. He smiled back.

Joey and Bobbie pawed through the packets. Joey picked out the Yankees players, Bobbie, the Dodgers.

"Who you gonna get?" he asked.

"Don't know."

More digging.

Then Joey unearthed a Jackie Robinson card. The serious face. The muscular arms. The ebony skin.

Joey thought about how Robinson had stood tall after being spiked by Enos Slaughter. About how he'd handled the black cat incident, with dignity. About his sixteen stolen bases. About his incredible batting average.

His hand closed over the card.

Wait a second! What was he doing? Bobbie would tease him to death if he chose Robinson. Was he turning traitor to his beloved Yankees?

No, of course not. He was still loyal to New York. Joe

DiMaggio was still his hero. It was just that Robinson was – well, so swell. Surreptitiously, Joey slid the Robinson card into his other hand, then continued sorting.

"Hmm . . ." Bobbie mused. She had Carl Furillo in one hand, Vic Lombardi in the other, and was looking back and forth between the two. "Lombardi," she decided. "Who're you getting?"

"Uh . . ." Joey snatched the first Yankees card that came to hand. "Snuffy Stirnweiss."

"Don't you already have him?"

"Uh . . . yeah. But I can always use another one. Can't have too many Snuffy Stirnweisses, that's what I always say."

She gave him an odd look, then glanced at his other hand. "What you got there?"

Joey's cheeks grew warm. "N-nothing." He tried to shove the Robinson card down in the box but Bobbie grabbed his hand and pried it open.

"Jackie Robinson!" She hooted. "Thought you were going to sneak that by me?"

"No, I –"

"I knew you were going soft on Brooklyn."

"Am not!" He dropped the Robinson card. "I was just moving it out of the way, that's all. I wouldn't buy a Dodgers card if you paid me."

Bobbie ignored him. "Hey, Mrs. Gershon, Joey's turning into a Dodgers fan."

"Oh, really?"

"Caught him red-handed with Jackie Robinson."

"No! I want Stirnweiss. See?"

"He just won't admit it," Bobbie said. "Probably got a secret stash of Dodgers cards in his room."

Laughing, Mrs. Gershon rang up their cards and the cigar for Zeyde. Once outside, Joey and Bobbie opened their packages. After comparing their players' stats, they broke up the gum and shoved all the pieces into their mouths. Sweetness burst over Joey's tongue as his jaws worked furiously, trying to chomp the brittle bits into a chewable mass. He blew his first, thick bubble, popped it and chewed again, making the gum more elastic. He stretched it with his tongue, preparing to blow a bubble.

Bobbie beat him. "Look," she said, her voice muffled, pointing at a big round pink bubble.

Joey's finger darted. *Splat!*

"Why, you –" She came after him.

Laughing, Joey turned aside, then blew his own bubble. Bobbie chased him, finger outstretched. He twisted one way, then the other. *Pop!* He ran straight into her finger.

"Ha!"

Down the street, around the corner, blowing and popping bubbles, running, spinning, laughing, faces getting stickier and stickier.

"Gotcha!"

"Gotcha back!"

Bobbie darted out of reach. "Missed me!" Then, in a singsong voice, "You like Jackie Robinson."

Joey felt his ears go warm. "I told you, I was putting it back —"

"Baloney. Admit it, you're coming over to Brooklyn."

"I am not!" Joey's whole face felt hot now. Spotting his chance, he darted in and smashed Bobbie's bubble, her biggest yet. Gum stretched practically to her ears.

"You'll pay for that!"

Laughing, Joey took off. But an uneasy feeling rippled through his stomach.

He'd *wanted* that Jackie Robinson card. What was happening to him?

CHAPTER

13

It had been raining for days.

The first day had been fun. Joey and Bobbie had gone out, despite the downpour, and built little dams out of sticks to hold back the water streaming into the gutters, counting to see how long it would take for the torrent of water to burst the dam and rush, frothing, on its way. They'd made it up to twenty.

But after they got in trouble for tracking mud all over the house, they were confined indoors.

They were miserable. Zeyde was grumpy. The only one who was happy was Aunt Frieda, because her boss, Mr. Turchin, had told her that she was doing such a good job, he had his eye on her for a promotion. This week she was being trained in new office duties. Ever since she'd received the news, she'd been standing a little taller, and she left each morning with a spring in her step, calling a cheery, "Have a good day!"

What Joey most definitely was not having was a good day. Or a good week. He'd had his fill of Go Fish and Crazy Eights, of checkers and Twenty Questions, of reading the newspaper and listening to the radio and rearranging his bulletin board. Finally, he said to Bobbie, "I don't care if there's a hurricane tomorrow, I'm going out."

The next day dawned overcast and gray. Heavy clouds tinged with black hovered in the sky, practically squatting on the buildings. But it wasn't raining. "Come on!" he said, grabbing Bobbie's arm.

He didn't have to say it twice. Bobbie was out the door almost before he was. They didn't bring their gloves and the bat; the field would be too muddy for baseball. No matter. They'd head there anyway, see if they could find the kids and figure out something else to do.

Sure enough, the usual gang was there. Vito and Grossie, Louie and Larry. Happily, no Eli and Tommy.

"Want to play hide and seek?" Bobbie suggested. "Or kick the can?"

No sooner were the words out of her mouth than a thunderclap sounded and the heavens opened. There was a chorus of groans as everyone ran to shelter under the maple tree. They peered out at the sheeting rain that ran in rivulets over the sodden earth.

"Maybe it won't last," Louie said.

"Yeah, sure," Larry said gloomily.

"Dodgers are playing today," Bobbie said. "If they don't get rained out."

Larry regarded the downpour. "Want to go to our house and listen to the game?"

Vito shook his head. "I can't stand to be inside for another minute."

"Me neither," Joey said.

"Wish we could *see* the game," Bobbie said.

"What, at Ebbets Field?" Grossie asked.

"Yeah."

Grossie laughed. "Me, too. Too bad we don't have money for tickets."

Bobbie sighed. "I know. But wouldn't it be swell?"

"Yeah . . . see Jackie get a hit," Louie said. "Maybe even steal a base."

"Why don't we go?" Joey said. As soon as the words were out of his mouth, he knew this might be trouble. But he was so bored and restless, he felt as if he could jump out of his skin. *And maybe*, he thought with a secret thrill, *I'll get to see Jackie Robinson play*. "Maybe we won't have to pay."

"You mean, *sneak* in?" Vito sounded amazed.

"Yeah. I can do it. Did it at Yankee Stadium."

"You did?" Larry and Louie said admiringly.

"Sure. Found a loose board under the left field bleachers. Saw the Yanks clobber the Orioles." Joey sighed. "Some game."

Bobbie looked excited. "You mean it, Joey?"

"Sure, what have we got to lose? Maybe we'll get kicked out. Maybe not. Better than standing here with nothing to do but get wet. Who wants to try?" Joey asked.

"Me!" Bobbie exclaimed.

"Me, too," Vito said.

Grossie looked nervous. "I don't know. My folks'd kill me if they knew."

"How are they going to know?" Bobbie said.

"If we get caught."

Joey flapped a hand. "We won't get caught. We find a crack, wait till the guards are looking the other way, then slip in. Find some empty seats way up high, nobody wants. It's a cinch."

"What d'you think, Lou?" Larry said.

"Daddy'll give us a licking for sure," his twin answered.

"I know."

"Let's do it anyway."

Larry shrugged. "Okay!"

Joey looked at Grossie. "What do you say, Grossie?"

"I don't know . . ."

"Come on, Grossie," Bobbie said. "It'll be fun. How else are you going to see a game?"

"We won't get caught, Grossie," Joey said. "Trust me."

The redhead wavered. "Oh, all right."

"Attaboy."

Running footsteps. Then two more figures darted under the tree. Fishkin and Flanagan. Eli sneered at Joey. "You came back for more? So I can finish the job?"

"Stuff it, Eli," Bobbie said. "We're not playing here anyway, so you can just save your threats."

"Yeah, we got something better to do," Vito said. "So there."

"Like what?"

"Like going to the Dodgers game," Louie said.

"You got tickets?" Eli said incredulously.

"We're going to sneak in," Larry said. "Joey's going to show us."

"*What!*"

"Yes, Joey," Bobbie snapped. "He's done it at Yankee Stadium and he's going to do it here."

"You're going to follow *him*?" Eli laughed. "You're cracked! You'll get caught for sure."

Grossie squirmed nervously.

"Will not," Joey said.

Tommy shook his head. "Might as well walk over to

the cops and say, 'Put the handcuffs on me now,'" he said. He stuck out his wrists and guffawed.

Eli turned to his friend. "Come on, Tommy, let's get away from these losers." He waved, fluttering his fingers. "Can't wait to see all of you in the slammer." Laughing, he and Tommy ran off.

"Good riddance," Vito muttered.

"Hey, look," Louie said. "It's stopped raining. Game'll be on."

"Must be a sign," Bobbie said with a grin. "Now, how are we going to get there? Anybody got money for the streetcar?"

Everybody checked pockets. Vito had thirty-five cents.

"Hey, Mr. Moneybags," Joey said, "spot us to streetcar fare?"

"Sure."

"All right, let's go!"

They got off at Flatbush Avenue, a couple of blocks from the stadium. As they approached it, Joey looked around eagerly. The others had probably been here before, but he never had, and any baseball stadium, even the Dodgers', was a treat to see.

EBBETS FIELD read huge letters over the massive entranceway. People milled about, waiting to pass through the turnstiles, crowding to see if any tickets were left.

From inside came the hum of many voices, the garbled echo of a loudspeaker, the peal of the organ.

"I'm scared," Grossie said.

"Don't worry," Joey said, though he didn't feel so confident anymore. Guards were posted on either side of the entrance, and the outside of the stadium looked as impregnable as a fortress. "Come on, let's scout the place out." Sauntering along the sidewalk as if he were just out for a stroll, he headed down a side street, the others in tow.

"Maybe this isn't such a good idea after all," Larry said.

"Take it easy, fellas," Bobbie said. "Joey'll figure it out."

Joey gulped. It had sounded easier standing under the maple tree. The wall along the first base line was solid. They continued around, along right field, then to center. Still no breaks.

"Darn stadium is built too good," Joey grumbled.

"I don't know about this," Grossie said. "Maybe we should just leave now —"

"Relax, Grossie, it'll be okay," Vito said. "Right, Joey?"

"Right."

Grossie took a deep breath. "All right . . . if you say so."

Joey led the group around to the left field wall. No breaks there. Then, as they turned the corner where the third base line slanted back toward the entrance, there was an opening. Two sawhorses made a *V* in front of a hole in the concrete, which was loosely covered with a sheet of plywood.

Joey made the thumbs-up sign.

"I told you Joey would get us in," Bobbie said.

Joey's heart was pounding. Trying to look casual, he glanced up and down the street. No guards. "All right, everybody, listen. I'll go in first, make sure it's okay. I'll signal the next person. We'll go in one at a time. If somebody comes along, don't panic. Just walk on like you're out for a stroll, got it?"

"Hole? What hole, officer?" Vito joked, and everyone laughed, even Grossie.

Looking right and left once more, Joey nudged the plywood aside. The opening was at ground level, about as big as a small child. Bobbie held the wood as Joey dropped to all fours and squeezed through.

"He's in!" Vito said.

A moment later, Joey's face appeared at the hole. "Perfect," he whispered. "We're under the bleachers at third base. No one's around. Who's next?"

"Me!" Bobbie said. A moment later, she squeezed through.

"Peanuts!" a vendor called above their heads. "Get ya peanuts!"

Bobbie looked up. "I can't believe I'm in Ebbets Field – for free!" Joey felt like a hero.

He motioned first Larry and then Louie inside.

"This is great," Louie said, straightening up. "You're swell, Joey."

Joey blushed. "Next," he whispered, and Vito easily slipped inside, joining the others under the bleachers.

Ladies and gentlemen, please rise for the national anthem, a voice boomed over the loudspeaker. Above them, the bleachers creaked.

Joey leaned through the opening. "Okay, Grossie. Last but not least."

Grossie bit his lip. "I don't know, Joey."

"Come on," Joey said.

"I don't think I can get through."

"Sure you can. It's bigger than you think. Come on."

The organ played the opening notes. The crowd began, *Oh, say can you see, by the dawn's early light . . .*

Grossie squeezed his head and shoulders through the opening. "I don't think –"

"What's the matter?" Bobbie and the others crowded over Joey's shoulder.

Whose broad stripes and bright stars, through the perilous fight . . .

"I can't do it," Grossie said. He was on the verge of tears.

"Sure you can, Grossie," Louie said.

"But what if –"

"You're okay, Grossie, just take it easy," Joey said soothingly.

But Grossie pulled his head back and disappeared.

And the rockets' red glare, the bombs bursting in air . . .

"Grossie!" Bobbie said sharply.

"Leave him to me," Joey said, and squeezed back outside.

Grossie shook his head nervously. "I'm sorry, Joey, I just —"

"That's okay." Joey patted him on the back. "But listen, it's great in there. The teams are on the field. The game's about to start. It'll be so much fun. What do you say?"

Grossie heaved a sigh. "Well . . . okay."

"Attaboy. Tell you what, I'll wait out here and keep watch for you, okay?"

"Okay."

. . . and the home of the brave. Cheers and applause. Above, the bleachers creaked as people sat down.

Grossie knelt and started squeezing through again.

Whew! Joey thought. Then, footsteps. Voices. He turned. Halfway down the block and moving fast in his direction, Eli. Tommy. And a security guard.

Eli was pointing. "There!" he shouted. "That's him."

"Oh, no," Joey said. "Come on, Grossie, move!"

On all fours, Grossie turned and looked over his shoulder. "Wha —" He froze.

"Hurry up, Grossie!"

Running footsteps. "Stop!" yelled the guard.

"*Move!*" Joey urged, but Grossie was frozen.

"What's going on?" Bobbie said from inside.

"Scatter, you guys!" Joey called.

A meaty hand landed on his shoulder. "Hold it. Just what do you think you're doing?"

The security guard was scowling. Grossie burst into tears.

"What's the matter?" Bobbie poked her head out. "Uh-oh."

"Run!" Joey whispered.

Before she could move, the guard yelled, "Charlie!"

From inside, a second security guard came running. "What the – oh, no, you don't."

Without letting go of Joey's collar, the first guard hauled a blubbering Grossie to his feet.

Play ball! the speaker boomed.

From what he could hear, Joey guessed that Charlie had corralled the four on the inside. As the guard dragged him away, Joey looked over his shoulder. There was no trace of Eli or Tommy.

The six of them sat alone in the office of the Chief of Security. After giving them a tongue-lashing – "If you punks don't straighten up, you'll end up behind bars!" –

he'd gone to call their parents, slamming the door behind him.

Now they waited. Grossie's blubbering subsided into noisy sniffles. Louie and Larry tapped their feet nervously. Vito looked grim, Bobbie, defiant.

Joey heaved a sigh. "Sorry, you guys."

"For what?" Vito said.

"Getting everybody in trouble."

"*You* didn't get us in trouble," Bobbie said.

"No, *I* did," Grossie said heavily.

They all turned to look at him.

"If I hadn't been so slow . . . if I hadn't been such a chicken and held things up –"

"Forget it, Grossie," Bobbie said. "It was just plain bad luck."

"That was no bad luck," Grossie returned. "Didn't you see?"

"See what?"

"Fishkin and Flanagan. They ratted on us," he said.

"*What!*" everyone said.

"I saw 'em. They were with the guard. Pointing at us. Right, Joey?"

"Right," Joey said grimly. He could just imagine how the two of them were laughing now.

"Those rats!" Bobbie said. "Why didn't you say anything, Joey?"

Joey shrugged. "What good would it do?" Eli and Tommy had done their work. Now the kids were in hot water. And, no matter what they said, it *was* his fault. They'd trusted him – and he'd let them down.

"You hellion!" Zeyde roared. They were back in the living room. His face was purple.

He glared at Joey. "I assume this was all your doing?"

Joey nodded.

"It was not!" Bobbie said.

Zeyde silenced her with a wave of his hand.

"But Zeyde, we all –"

"Quiet!" He turned back to Joey. "First you get into fights, then you go on a tirade in front of the whole neighborhood, now this. How many times will you shame us? How many?"

Joey said nothing.

Zeyde grabbed him by the arm and marched him into the kitchen. He turned Joey over his knee and spanked him, hard.

Joey didn't cry.

Then Zeyde did the same thing to Bobbie.

She didn't cry, either.

The two of them were sent to their rooms.

Joey lay on his side, his bottom stinging, waiting for the summons. Any minute now, he expected to be told to pack his things. And if that wasn't bad enough, it wasn't just himself that he'd got into trouble this time, but his friends. Would Zeyde even give him time to say goodbye to them, to tell them how sorry he was, before he shipped him out?

A door opened downstairs – Aunt Frieda home from work. His stomach in a knot, Joey glided to his door, opened it a crack, and listened as Zeyde filled her in on the escapade.

"Oh, dear," Aunt Frieda said. But to Joey's amazement, she didn't sound all that upset.

"Oh, dear?" Zeyde repeated. "Is that all you can say?"

"Well, what should I do? Weep and wail? It was only a silly prank –"

"A prank? To break into a stadium illegally –"

"Oh, come on, Daddy, don't get carried away. Sure, it's naughty, but what children aren't naughty? Didn't you do stuff like that when you were their age? Steal a pack of bubble gum? Tell a fib?"

"I never broke into Ebbets Field," Zeyde said righteously.

"That's because there *was* no Ebbets Field."

"Frieda!" Zeyde sounded shocked, and Joey had to chuckle. Aunt Frieda was getting bold in her old age! "But it's not just one little prank," Zeyde went on. "It's one thing after another –"

"Yes, it is. I've been thinking about that. And you know what I think, Daddy?"

"What?"

"*You* make him worse."

"What!"

Aunt Frieda's voice faltered, but she went on. "You do. All this spanking and punishing and yelling –"

"Don't start in with that again, Frieda. At least I know how to discipline a wayward child."

"Like Becky?"

A pause. "Yes, like Becky!"

"And what did the discipline do, Daddy? It drove her away! I remember when you caught Becky with a face covered in makeup –"

"Like a tramp!" Zeyde said angrily.

"And you yelled and carried on. But did she stop? No! She did worse – started smoking and drinking."

"That wasn't my fault!"

"And when she started sneaking out to dances, you grounded her for weeks – so she stayed out later."

"I didn't punish her hard enough, that was the problem."

"No, it wasn't. The punishing *was* the problem. It didn't work with Becky and it's not working with Joey either."

"How dare you put the blame on me!" Zeyde shouted.

"The problem is that boy. He's wild and undisciplined, and he's getting worse —" Zeyde's voice broke for a moment, but then he went on angrily, "And if he doesn't straighten out, I'm sending him —"

"Over my dead body!"

Shocked silence. "What!"

"You heard me."

"Frieda . . ."

"I mean it, Daddy. You think about it. Goodnight."

Zeyde made a little noise of protest, but he didn't say anything. Aunt Frieda started up the stairs, and Joey quickly ducked back into his room.

Over my dead body. She'd fought for him! She wanted him! She wouldn't let Zeyde send him away. Joey fell back on his bed, oblivious to his sore bottom, feeling safe for the first time since he'd arrived.

But then a chill chased away the warm feeling. Aunt Frieda might want him to stay, she might have stood up to Zeyde this time, but everyone knew that Zeyde was in charge. What he said, went. And he had just said: *If he doesn't straighten out, I'm sending him —*

The fear of not knowing where he might end up went deeper now. Because he really loved it here, loved Bobbie, loved Aunt Frieda, loved his friends, even loved Brooklyn — and he wanted to stay.

And it all might be taken away.

CHAPTER

14

Joey and Bobbie were confined to their rooms all that day and all of the next. Aunt Frieda brought their meals on a tray, and although she seemed sympathetic, she didn't let them out. The second day was worse than the first. Joey thought he'd die of boredom. He looked out the window. He rearranged his Yankees cards on the bulletin board. He looked out the window some more. He thought about sneaking out again, but remembering what Zeyde had said, decided he'd better mind his *p*'s and *q*'s.

Downstairs, the radio blared big band music. Above that, Aunt Frieda clanged pots in the kitchen. It was Friday. Shabbas. Joey knew the word now. And the routine – the candles, the chanting, the bread, the wine.

But that was about all he knew. He still didn't know the prayers. He frowned, remembering how Zeyde had

yelled at him that first Shabbas. At least his grandfather
had left him alone on the Shabbases since then. For the
last few Fridays, Joey had stood there like a dummy while
the rest of them chanted. Zeyde hadn't yelled; he'd just
ignored him.

An idea struck.

Nah, it wouldn't work anyway.

But if it did, maybe it would change Zeyde's mind and
make him like Joey better. *Maybe,* Joey thought, *Zeyde
wouldn't be too ashamed to take me to* schul.

Joey slipped into Bobbie's room and carefully shut the
door. She was lying on her back, hands beneath her head,
staring at the ceiling. She raised her head, brightened.
"You're not supposed to be in here," she whispered.

"I know, but I'm going crazy," he answered.

She lay back. "Tell me about it."

Joey sat on the end of her bed. They were quiet for a
moment. Offhandedly, he said, "You know those prayers?"

She raised herself onto her elbows. "What prayers?"

"The Friday night ones."

"The Shabbas prayers? What about 'em?"

He lowered his eyes. "Will you teach me?"

"You want me to teach you the Shabbas prayers?" she
asked, surprised.

"Yeah."

She hesitated. Joey searched her face for any sign that she was laughing at him. But she wasn't. "How come?"

"So I . . . I just do."

"Right now?"

"Yeah."

Bobbie grinned. "Sure. Beats staring at the ceiling." She pushed herself up, sat cross-legged facing him. "Okay, here's how it goes. *Bah-ruch.*" She made a noise deep in her throat. "Say that."

"*Bah-roo —*"

"No, not *bah-roo. Bah-ruch.*"

"*Bah-ruh.*" Joey made a breathy sound at the end of the word.

Bobbie shook her head. "Try again."

"*Bah-ruck.*"

She rolled her eyes. "Not *bah-ruck.* It's not a 'k.' *Bah-ruch.* Use your throat."

"I am!"

"Keep your voice down!" she snapped in a loud whisper.

"I am using my throat," he whispered back.

"You are not. *Bah-ruch.*"

"*Bah-rugh.*"

"For crying out loud, you sound like a tugboat. '*Bah-rugh. Bah-rugh.*'" She imitated a foghorn.

"Shut up."

She giggled. "Come on. *Bah-ruch.*"

"*Bah-ruck-h.*" He exhaled at the end.

"No! Sheesh, what's wrong with you?"

"Nothing! Must be the way you're teaching me."

"Is not."

"Oh, never mind." Joey started to get up. "Who cares about being Jewish, anyway?"

She pulled him down. "Hold on. Here, think of it like this. You got a big gob in your throat and you're trying to hawk it up."

Joey gave her an incredulous look.

"Really. That's what it's like. A big gob of spit. Come on. *Chgk. Chgk.*" She made a throat-clearing noise.

Joey was sure she was pulling his leg. But she looked dead serious. Tentatively, he made a noise in his throat. "*Hkhh . . .*"

Bobbie rolled her eyes. "You'll never get it up that way."

"*Chk.*" A little louder.

"Come on, a great big gob. Hawk it!"

"*Chgk.*"

"Deeper."

"*CHGK. CHGK.*"

"That's it! Do it again!"

"*Bah-ruch. Bah-RUCH. Bah-RUCH.*"

"You got it!"

"*Bah-ruch, bah-ruch, bah-ruch,*" Joey said happily. "What a swell language. You get to make rude noises and you don't even get in trouble."

Bobbie laughed. "Okay. Here we go. *Bah-ruch ah-taw ah-do-noy . . .*"

"Adenoid? Ain't that something in your throat?"

Bobbie burst out laughing. "Not adenoid, you dummy –"

"Hey, who you calling a dummy?"

"Adenoid," she repeated, slapping her knee.

"All right, if you're so smart, what is it, then?"

"*AH-DO-NOY,*" she said slowly. "It means God."

"Oops."

She stifled a giggle. "It's all right. God can probably take a joke."

"I hope so."

She taught him the next several words. When they came to "*meh-lech,*" Joey said, "Wait. That's one of those gob ones, isn't it?"

"Yeah."

They continued until Joey learned the final words, "*l'had-leek nair shel Shabbas.*" He ran through the whole prayer a few times, twice with coaching, once by himself.

"Good," Bobbie said.

"What's it mean, anyway?"

"It means we're thanking God for telling us to light the Shabbas candles. That's what *l'had-leek nair shel Shabbas* means – to kindle the lights of the Sabbath."

Joey nodded. He wouldn't admit it, but it made a lovely picture in his mind, Aunt Frieda kindling the lights of the Sabbath with that lacy white scarf on her dark hair.

"Now you got to learn the other two."

"What other two?"

"The other two prayers, over the bread and the wine."

Joey groaned. "This is a lot of work."

"Don't worry, they're mostly the same. There's only new stuff at the end."

Bobbie started again, coaching Joey through the two new endings, one for the bread, and one for the wine. He practiced, making great hawking noises every time he came to a gob word.

Finally, after hearing him recite all three prayers with no mistakes, Bobbie declared he was ready.

Joey grinned. *Hope it works*, he thought. But he didn't say it out loud.

Staring at the candlesticks, Joey jammed his hands into the pockets of his good trousers. He'd wet down his hair and tried to tame the curls. He'd put on a clean polo shirt. He'd even cleaned his fingernails.

The smells of roast beef and carrots and potatoes were wafting out of the kitchen, filling the dining room with a delicious fragrance, but Joey scarcely noticed. His heart was pounding too hard.

Aunt Frieda draped the kerchief over her head. *Kindle the lights of the Sabbath*, Joey thought, and relaxed a little. As Aunt Frieda began to sing, and Bobbie's and Zeyde's voices lifted to join hers, Joey began, quietly, "*Ba-ruch ah-taw ah-do-noy . . .*" Hesitantly, then a little louder, "*eh-lo-hay-nu me-lech ha-olam . . .*"

Aunt Frieda stopped, turned, and looked at Joey.

Had he made a mistake?

But no, a smile was lighting up her face, and it stayed there as she continued, "*ah-sher kiddish-aw-nu b'mitz-vo-sav . . .*"

Joey smiled back, still singing. Then he noticed that Zeyde was staring at him with a look that Joey couldn't read. The candles flickered, and for a moment Joey thought that his grandfather's eyes glittered as if they were wet. Zeyde turned front again and continued chanting.

They finished the first prayer. Zeyde lifted the *challah* and started saying the prayer over the bread. Joey joined in. Then the prayer over the wine.

As soon as the last note faded, Aunt Frieda grabbed Joey. "Joey, that was wonderful! All three prayers, and perfect, too! I'm so proud of you." She hugged him – and for the first time, he hugged her back. God, it felt good.

Her arm still around Joey, Aunt Frieda turned to her father. "Daddy, did you hear that? Wasn't it a wonderful surprise? Aren't you proud of him?"

Zeyde looked at Joey with an unaccustomed softness in his eyes. Finally a small smile curved his lips. "Very good, Joey."

"It was fantastic!" Aunt Frieda said. "Did you teach him, Bobbie?"

"Yup. But it was his idea. He learned good, didn't he?"

"Well, Bobbie," Aunt Frieda said dryly. "He learned well."

Bobbie flapped her hand. "Oh, Mama, who cares? He did great."

Aunt Frieda laughed. "Yes, he did. Absolutely great!" She hugged Joey again. "Now, sit down, everybody, and I'll get dinner."

Joey repeated Zeyde's words to himself. *Very good.* They were the first words of praise Joey had heard from his mouth. And Zeyde had even smiled. Not a grin, not even a big smile, but still, a smile. A feeling of relief swept over him.

But it was more than relief, he realized with surprise as Aunt Frieda came in with a platter of roast beef and started serving. It was pleasure. He'd made Zeyde happy, and that felt good.

Right away, Joey caught himself. It didn't mean that Zeyde was proud of him, or wouldn't still send him away – so he'd better not get all excited.

15

The next day, Joey and Bobbie headed for the vacant lot. Joey, delighted to be freed at last, chattered away about hitting and fielding and pitching – until he noticed that Bobbie wasn't responding. In fact, now that he thought about it, she hadn't said a word since they'd left the house. She was marching along in silence, her glove clenched in her fist, her mouth set in a grim line.

Joey stopped, mid-sentence. Maybe, despite Bobbie's earlier protestations that the Ebbets Field fiasco hadn't been his fault, she really was mad at him for getting them all in trouble.

Joey risked a glance at his cousin. Her chin was set, her eyes fixed straight ahead. He swallowed. That must be it. And who could blame her? It had been his idea, after all.

He was trying to work up the courage to ask her if that was what she was mad about, when they turned the corner, and there, walking toward them, gloves in hand, were Grossie and Vito.

"Hey, fellas," Joey said.

"Hey, Joey, hey, Bobbie," Vito said. Both fell into step without the usual banter or discussion of the Dodgers. Both sets of eyes were narrowed, both pairs of lips were compressed into thin lines. Neither looked at him. They marched along, silent and grim.

They must be mad, too, Joey thought, his heart sinking. With each step, he felt worse.

As they headed for the vacant lot, Louie and Larry joined them.

Again, the furious looks, the angry strides.

Now Joey was convinced that they were mad at him. And why not? They'd probably all gotten punished, just for going along with his bone-headed idea.

Maybe, he thought nervously, *they're so fed up that they don't want to be my friends anymore. And just when I finally had some real pals, too.*

Well, even if they were about to ditch him, he had to let them know how sorry he was. He gulped. "Say, listen, fellas, I'm really –"

He stopped. Eli and Tommy were in the lot, throwing a ball back and forth.

The group on the sidewalk formed a tight flank.

Eli rolled his eyes. "What is it with you guys? Do we got to pound you again? I told you, the nigger can't play."

No, Joey thought with dismay. *Not again.* Now he'd have to fight, and then he'd get in trouble, and then he'd get punished, and Zeyde —

Vito stepped forward, hands on hips. "You're wrong, Fishkin," he said. "Joey *can* play. Right here. On this lot. With us."

"You must like getting beat up, Marconi."

Tommy flexed his fists. "Guess he didn't get enough last time, huh, Eli?"

"Guess not."

Before Joey understood what was happening, Louie stepped forward, too. "Yeah, Fishkin, he can."

"Starting right now," Larry stated, joining his twin.

Joey was stunned.

"Oh, yeah? Is that so?" Eli said. He loosened his shoulders. Tommy cracked his knuckles. They both moved toward the three boys on the sidewalk.

Joey could just picture the massacre. All of it on his conscience. "Listen, fellas, don't be silly, you don't have to —"

He stopped short as Grossie stepped forward. *Grossie!* With his hands in fists! "Yeah, you rat finks!" he shouted. "And you know what? *You two* can't play."

Eli and Tommy burst out laughing. "*We* can't play?" Eli repeated. "Says who?"

"Me," said Vito, taking a stand.

"Me!" added Larry.

"And me!" said Louie.

"ME!" It was Grossie!

Before Joey knew what was happening, all four of them had flung themselves on Eli and Tommy.

Joey could hardly believe it. They weren't mad, they were sticking up for him! He felt a short-lived surge of joy – just before he realized that they were going to get killed. He had to stop them!

"No, you guys, don't!" he yelled. Ignoring him, they rained punches on Fishkin and Flanagan.

Throwing off their attackers, Eli and Tommy crouched back to back in fighting stance. "Come on then, you wimps," Eli taunted.

Joey shot a look at Bobbie. They couldn't just stand by and watch their friends get annihilated! But then, to his astonishment, he saw that his buddies were holding their own! Eli and Tommy were bigger and stronger, but the smaller boys' punches were coming from all directions. The bullies turned from one to another in confusion.

The four friends were actually doing some damage. Vito landed several punches while his quick feet danced him out of range of the larger boys' jabs. Louie didn't throw many punches, but he made sure each one counted and managed to bloody a startled Eli's nose. With a mighty shove, Larry pushed Tommy to the ground. Grossie, too slow and heavy to be much of a fighter, had a look of determination Joey had never seen before. He backed up, took a running start, and hurled himself through the air, plowing into Eli. Eli landed on top of Tommy, and Grossie sat down hard, straddling the two. The boys beneath him struggled in vain. Grossie lifted his bottom and bounced down.

His head thrown back, Joey laughed. "Go, Grossie! Give it to 'em!"

Grossie plopped down hard. And again.

"Unnhh! Get off, you tub!"

"Oooohh!"

"'Nuff," Eli finally called out.

Tommy's muffled cry of "Uncle!" ended it. Brushing off his hands like a western sheriff, Grossie rolled off.

Eli and Tommy struggled to their feet. A trail of dust-caked blood ran from Eli's nose.

"You get the message, you rat finks?" Larry said. "Now, get lost."

"And don't come back," Vito snapped. "Ever."

Eli and Tommy picked up their gloves, darting nervous looks over their shoulders. They edged between the twins, started running, and disappeared around the corner.

As his friends brushed themselves off and put their Brooklyn caps back on, Joey looked from one to another. Seeing their blood and bruises and rips and welts, he suddenly felt himself choking up. "Thanks, fellas," he said in a husky voice. "I thought . . . oh, never mind." He swallowed. "Thanks."

"That's okay," Vito said. "It was the least we could do."

"Yeah," Grossie said. "It wasn't just for you. It was for us, too. Should've done it long ago." He patted his middle. "Finally found my secret weapon," he said proudly, and everyone laughed.

Joey studied his friends again. "Hey, what are we standing around for? The field's ours. Let's play ball!"

Everyone jumped into action.

"Choose 'em up!"

"Joey!" the cry rang out.

"Joey!"

"Joey . . ."

16

J oey was the first one downstairs the next morning. The newspaper was still on the doormat. He brought it into the kitchen, poured himself a glass of milk, and pulled out the sports section.

Automatically he started turning to the Yankees' news, but his eye was caught by the front page headline.

New York Daily News, August 2, 1947
CINCINNATI, OHIO – Jackie's 9th Inning Single
Puts Dodgers Past Redlegs, 4-3

Boy, that Robinson! Joey thought. In spite of himself, he kept reading.

The rookie has done it again. With the score tied 3-all in the top of the ninth, Jackie Robinson slapped a line drive to right field, driving home Dixie Walker with the go-ahead run. Then he made an over-the-head catch to rob Augie Galan of what looked like a sure base hit to end the game and hand Brooklyn a 4-3 victory.

Footsteps.

Quickly, Joey tried to turn the page but the sheets were stuck together. He wet his finger. Come on!

"Hiya," Bobbie said, coming into the kitchen. "We win?"

"How should I know? I don't read Dodgers' news."

"Looks like that's exactly what you were doing."

"Was not. The pages're stuck, that's all."

"I bet."

"They are!" Joey put his finger between the pages and ripped a shred of newspaper at the corner. "See? Told you. They were stuck. I just couldn't turn the page."

Her nose in the refrigerator, Bobbie said, "So, did we win?"

"Four-three."

She pulled her head out, grinning triumphantly. "See? You *were* reading it."

Joey blushed. "I just happened to notice the headline."

She sniffed loudly. "I smell a Dodgers fan."

"You're cracked."

"Sniff, sniff."

"Aw, get lost." Joey pushed the sports section at her. "Here, take the stupid paper. See if I care." He left the kitchen before she could make any more smart remarks.

On his way upstairs, he stopped. Shoot! He still didn't know if the Yankees had won.

A couple of days later, Joey was in the kitchen clipping an article, when Bobbie walked in.

"What're you cutting?" she asked.

"Oh, just another Yankees win for a change," he said, pretending to be bored. "Nine-six over the Red Sox. Fifth in a row."

"Who cares?" She nudged him with her shoulder. "Out of the way, I can't see the Dodgers' score. Hey, look!" She pointed at the opposite page. " 'Dodgers Win Fourth Straight, Doubling Cards, 6-3,' " she read aloud. "Ha-ha, you think you're so great."

"We got a better record."

"We're coming on strong. Four in a row. And look at this." She pointed to a second article. There was a picture of Jackie Robinson, and above it the headline read, "Robinson in Line for Rookie of the Year Honors." Bobbie rolled her eyes. "What do they mean, in line for? *Of course* he's rookie of the year."

Joey's eyes darted to the article. It began:

Jackie Robinson is having a year that any veteran ball player would be proud of, but for a rookie it's nothing short of miraculous. . . .

He tore his eyes away. "Yeah, well, talk to me when you've got a record of 77 and 40." He touched a finger to his temple. "Oh, wait. You can't. You've already got 46 losses. Too bad."

"Stuff it," Bobbie said, leaning over Joey's shoulder to read the article.

With great fanfare, Joey finished cutting out the Yankees article, then put away the scissors. He poured cereal into bowls for himself and Bobbie and brought them to the table.

"Thanks," she said, still reading about Robinson.

Joey sat across from her and tried to read the article upside down. Finally Bobbie finished eating and folded the paper. "We're going to win the pennant, I can feel it."

"*Brooklyn?* Dream on."

"Oh, shush." She took the two bowls to the sink. "Want to go out and practice pitching?"

"Sure."

"Okay. I've got to go upstairs for a minute. Be right down."

"You done with the paper?" Joey asked casually.

"Yup."

"Has . . . uh . . . Zeyde seen it yet?"

"Yeah, I think so. Why?"

"Oh . . . no reason."

Bobbie gave him an odd look. Joey waited until he heard her footsteps on the upstairs landing. He retrieved the scissors and turned back to the Robinson article.

Should he?

Why not? It was no crime, after all.

But Robinson was a Dodger.

But this didn't have anything to do with the Dodgers. The Dodgers could go hang themselves. He only cared about Robinson. 'Cause he was a rookie and he was having a terrific season. He had stood up to the jerks and kept his promise and his pride, and was proving that a Negro could play with anybody.

But –

He wanted that article. Just like he'd wanted that baseball card in Gershon's, the one he'd missed out on because of Bobbie's eagle eyes. Well, she was nowhere around now. . . .

Quickly, he snipped out the story, stuffed the rest of the newspaper in the garbage, and ran upstairs.

"You ready, Joey?" Bobbie called from her room.

"Be right with you," he called back, closing his door.

Now what? Where was he going to put it? It had to be where nobody could see it, because if Bobbie or Aunt

Frieda or Zeyde found out he'd clipped a Jackie Robinson story, he'd never hear the end of it. Where . . . ? His eyes darted around the room.

"Joey?"

"One minute!"

His eyes lighted on his bed. Under his pillow? No, it could fall on the floor. *In* the pillowcase. Yes, that was it. He slipped the article inside the pillowcase, under the pillow. Smoothed the bedding. You'd never know it was there.

"Where are you already?"

"Coming!"

Over the next week, Joey clipped more articles about Jackie Robinson. "Speedy Robinson Steals Twentieth Base." "Robinson Homer Powers Surging Dodgers Past Phillies." "Manager Shotten Says: 'Rookie Has It All.'"

Each time, Joey spirited the article upstairs and stuffed it in his pillowcase.

"Jackie Goes Four for Four."

Each time, he told himself that he was just interested in Robinson as a baseball player.

"Robinson's Base Running Is Stellar."

It had nothing to do with the Dodgers. He was just as devoted to the Yankees as ever. The fact that the first thing he did in the morning was to check for news about Robinson didn't mean a thing.

"Robinson Ignores Taunts, Clouts Winning Run in St. Louis."

And the growing lump under his pillow was definitely, positively, absolutely NOT a collection.

CHAPTER
17

Several days later, Joey came downstairs, wearing his many-times-mended T-shirt and a pair of blue shorts. It was Friday, Aunt Frieda's day off, and she was in the kitchen, beating cake batter.

Reaching high into the cupboard for a glass, Joey felt her eyes on him. He turned to find her gazing at him thoughtfully.

"What?"

"Your shirt's small. You've grown."

Joey looked down. True enough, an inch of skin showed between his shirt and his shorts. "Guess so."

"Put on weight, too. Got a little tummy now."

"I do not!"

She laughed. "That's *good*, Joey. You're not such a scrawny little chicken, like when you first came."

"Aunt Frieda!" he said, outraged. But he laughed with her, then bent over to tie his sneaker. As he wiggled his foot, there was a *r-r-rip* sound, and his big toe poked through the canvas.

Aunt Frieda frowned.

Uh-oh, Joey thought.

Bobbie came into the kitchen, dressed in a polo shirt and shorts, baseball glove in hand. "Ready, Joey?"

"Bobbie, go get changed," Aunt Frieda said.

"Why?"

"We're going shopping."

"Shopping?" A horrified look.

"Shopping," Aunt Frieda repeated. "Joey doesn't have a decent thing to wear, he's bursting through his shoes, and you can both use some new school clothes."

"School!" Bobbie wailed. "Mama! How can you even mention that word?"

But Joey's heart leaped. He couldn't remember ever having new school clothes.

"Go on, Bobbie, put on a skirt and blouse."

"Ma-*ma*!"

"You heard me. Shorts are fine for playing, but I'm not taking you on Utica Avenue dressed like a boy."

With a huff, Bobbie stomped out. Quickly, Aunt Frieda finished mixing the cake and slid it into the oven, calling out to Zeyde to keep an eye on it. Then she ran upstairs to change out of her housedress.

Fifteen minutes later they headed out, Bobbie in a red-and-white striped sundress – and her worn Keds – Aunt Frieda in a slim brown skirt and sleeveless white blouse, her hair tucked under a straw sunhat, Joey in a clean polo shirt and shorts. The heels of her brown-and-white pumps tapping on the sidewalk, Aunt Frieda smiled, first at one, then the other. "Guess what."

"What?"

"Remember I told you Mr. Turchin was considering me for a promotion? Well, I got it – and a raise!"

"Wow! That's swell, Aunt Frieda," Joey said

"I told you you were good, Mama," Bobbie said.

Aunt Frieda smiled. "Well . . . I guess Mr. Turchin thought so."

"You're too modest," Bobbie said. "What's your new job?"

"Office manager."

"That sounds important," Joey said.

"It's more work, that's for sure," Aunt Frieda said. "I'm in charge of three people now." She put her hand on her chest. "Imagine, *me* a boss."

"Why not?" Bobbie said. "You know what you're doing."

"I suppose I do," Aunt Frieda said. Then, "Sure I do!"

She giggled. "And you know what? Since I'm earning more, I just might treat myself to a new dress, or maybe that pretty hat I saw in Goldblatt's window."

"Big spender," Bobbie teased.

Aunt Frieda laughed. She grabbed their hands and swung them. Joey swung back.

They turned onto Utica Avenue, and who should be coming down the street toward them but Eli Fishkin and Tommy Flanagan.

Uh-oh, Joey thought, dreading the idea of being called names – or even having to fight – in front of Aunt Frieda. But the two boys quickly crossed the street.

Joey and Bobbie looked at each other across Aunt Frieda and burst out laughing.

"What?" Aunt Frieda said.

"Nothing," Bobbie said, giggling.

Aunt Frieda looked from one to the other, shaking her head. "Kids!" she said, but she let it drop.

The cousins were still giggling as Aunt Frieda steered them into Grossman's Children's Wear. A portly man with wavy, reddish-blond hair approached them.

"Hello, Frieda, how are you?"

"Fine, Harry, how are you?"

He turned to Bobbie. "Roberta, you've shot up so, I wouldn't have known you."

"Hi, Mr. Grossman."

Then to Joey. "And you must be Joey. Freddie's told me all about you."

Joey smiled uncertainly. "Freddie?" He took another look at the man. The chubby cheeks, the sprinkle of freckles. "Oh – Grossie." Then he clapped a hand over his mouth.

The man laughed and his stomach bounced. "That's all right. They called me Grossie when I was a kid, too, didn't they, Frieda?"

"Sure did."

"You knew each other?" Bobbie asked.

Aunt Frieda nodded. "We even dated in high school."

"Dated!" Bobbie said.

"You betcha. Your mama was real sweet on me, too."

"Mama!" Bobbie said with a mortified look.

Mr. Grossman laughed. "Until your daddy came along, that is. Then it was all over for me."

"If you . . . if Mama . . ." Bobbie said, looking perplexedly from one to the other, ". . . I wouldn't be here!"

"Or Grossie – I mean, Freddie – either," Joey put in, trying to figure out what it would be like to have some weird combination of Bobbie and Grossie for a cousin.

"Right. So it's good things worked out the way they did," Mr. Grossman said. "Now, what can I do for you?"

In and out of dressing rooms, then over to the shoe rack at the back of the store. Bobbie complained about every blouse and skirt and dress she had to try on, insisted on the plainest designs, refused anything with a bow or lace or flowers. But Joey loved everything – the soft cotton of the striped T-shirts, the crisp collars of the new button-down shirts, one a blue-and-white check, the other brown with a thin beige stripe, the sharp creases of the two pairs of pants – one brown and one blue – the gleam of his black-and-white Buster Brown saddle shoes with black-and-white laces. Aunt Frieda even bought them each a new pair of Keds, red for Bobbie, navy blue for Joey, which they put on right away. Laden with packages, they set off down the street.

Joey was surprised he didn't sprout wings and fly away. So many swell new things. He'd just received more in an hour than Mama had bought him in a year. And it wasn't just the *things*. It was being out with Bobbie and Aunt Frieda, greeting people, hearing the car horns and the chatter and the streetcar rumble, seeing what was playing at the Rialto, thinking about how he'd dirty up his new Keds the next time he and the fellas played ball.

They crossed the street. On the corner was Gershon's. Bobbie tugged Aunt Frieda's arm. "Since you just put us through torture, Mama, don't you think you should make it up to us with ice-cream sodas?"

"That wasn't torture –" Joey began, but Bobbie poked him.

Aunt Frieda smiled. "Oh, I suppose you could twist my arm."

While she picked up some bath powder, Joey followed Bobbie to the soda fountain at the rear of the store. They sat on red-cushioned stools with chrome pedestals. Joey gave his seat a twirl. Last time he'd been to a soda fountain was a year or so ago. Mama had been in one of her good times. Joey remembered what fun they'd had, spinning on the stools. He'd had what he always had: a chocolate ice cream with chocolate soda. Mama had had coffee and chocolate, her favorite.

"Hey, Bobbie, got a date?" a voice said.

Behind the counter was a teenager in a white short-sleeved shirt with *Gershon's* stitched on the pocket, a red bow tie, and a white soda jerk cap. He held an ice-cream scoop.

"Oh, Lenny, shush," Bobbie returned. "This is no date, it's my cousin."

"Your cousin, huh? And does your cousin have a name?"

"Joey. Joey Sexton," Bobbie said. "This is Lenny Gershon, Joey, and he's a pain in the neck."

Joey saw the resemblance to Mrs. Gershon in his green eyes. "But I make the best ice-cream sodas in Brooklyn, don't I, Bobbie?"

"Yeah," Bobbie admitted.

Lenny grinned. "Now, what can I get you?"

"A soda. Vanilla ice cream with chocolate for me," Bobbie said. "How about you, Joey?"

"Chocolate-chocolate."

"A chocolate nut, huh?" Lenny said.

Joey smiled. "Yup."

Aunt Frieda came over and sat on the stool next to Joey.

"Hi, Mrs. Rosen, what'll it be?" Lenny said.

"Chocolate soda with coffee ice cream."

Just like Mama.

"Coming right up."

Joey watched as Lenny chose three tall glasses and fixed the sodas. He topped them with whipped cream and maraschino cherries, put the glasses on small round saucers, placed a straw and a long-handled spoon on each dish, and lifted them to the counter.

"Ta-da!" he said.

Joey dug in. Ah, the froth of the whipped cream and the sweetness of the maraschino cherry, the nose-tickling tartness of the soda and the velvet richness of the chocolate . . .

For a while there was no sound but the slurp of soda and the clink of spoons on glasses.

"Good, Joey?" Aunt Frieda said.

Joey just sighed. Several minutes later, he tilted his glass to catch the last drops of soda, then put down his spoon.

"Want another, Joey?" Aunt Frieda asked.

He stared at her. "Could I?"

"Why not?"

'Cause there's not enough money, he almost said, then caught himself. "Sure!"

"Me, too!" Bobbie said, tugging her mama's sleeve.

Fifteen minutes later, they both pushed their plates away.

"I don't think I can move," Bobbie said.

"I'll never eat again," Joey said.

"That's a shame," Aunt Frieda said. "We're having roast turkey and mashed potatoes and lemon cake for dinner."

"Well . . . I might be able to manage by then," Joey said.

"I don't know, Joey, I wouldn't want you to get sick," Aunt Frieda teased.

No roast turkey and mashed potatoes and cake! Then Joey saw that she was hiding a smile. "Don't do that to me, Aunt Frieda!"

She ruffled his hair.

When they went up to the front counter to pay, Mrs. Gershon greeted them. She touched Aunt Frieda's hand. "I'm so sorry about Becky, Frieda."

Aunt Frieda's eyes filled with tears. "Thanks, Doris."

Mrs. Gershon nodded at Joey. "He's the image of her, though, isn't he?

"Isn't he just?" Aunt Frieda said, gazing at Joey as she wiped her eyes.

"Remember how she used to hate her hair?" Mrs. Gershon said.

Aunt Frieda laughed. "Do I! She used to say, 'Make it lie down, Frieda, make it lie down!'"

"And all the girls drooled with envy over those curls."

Aunt Frieda smiled. "Did we ever."

"Remember that time she made me iron it?" Mrs. Gershon said.

"*Iron* it?" Bobbie asked.

"Yes," Aunt Frieda said, laughing. "Doris – Mrs. Gershon – was babysitting, and Becky's hair was particularly wild that day. Knowing Becky, she probably hadn't combed it in days. Anyway, she begged Mrs. Gershon to iron it flat –"

"And I said, 'I don't think this is a good idea, Becky.'"

"But you couldn't say no to Becky; no one could."

Mrs. Gershon chuckled. "So I got out the iron and she laid her head down on the ironing board –"

"And there was this horrible burning smell –"

The two women were guffawing.

"And her hair stuck straight out, all frizzled –"

"And she went and washed it and it went back all curly again –"

"And the next day Mama said, 'What's the matter with my iron? It smells funny.'"

Joey and Bobbie joined the laughter.

"Oh, God," Aunt Frieda said, hand on her chest, "what a character."

Another customer came along, so they said their good-byes and left. As soon as they got outside, Joey said, "Aunt Frieda? Tell me more about Mama."

She smiled down at him. "Oh, Joey, she was the prettiest girl in Brooklyn."

"You're pretty, Mama," Bobbie said loyally.

Aunt Frieda smiled. "Thank you, Bobbele." She turned back to Joey. "But not like Becky. She was something special. She just had a spark. She was always laughing, always making other people laugh."

"How?" Joey asked.

"Oh, she'd clown around, wearing our mama's hats, or Zeyde's big shoes, and sing silly songs. And the practical jokes . . ." Aunt Frieda shook her head. "One time, I guess I was about sixteen, so she would have been thirteen, I had my first tube of lipstick – Fire Engine Red, it was called, oh, what a color, like ripe tomatoes, I was so proud of it. I wasn't even allowed to wear it yet, but I used to take it out and look at it. The day came, I had my first date – it was with Harry Grossman, in fact – and Mama said I could wear my lipstick. At last! Carefully, carefully, I put it on. But it felt funny, kind of wet, so I reached out with my tongue. *Blech!* I spat all over the place. Becky had put ketchup in my lipstick tube!"

The three of them roared.

"What a devil," Aunt Frieda went on. "How she used to make Daddy laugh."

"Daddy? You mean Zeyde?" Joey said, incredulous.

Aunt Frieda nodded. "She was his girl. *Oy vey*, how he adored her. I was Mama's favorite because I was like her, quiet and sweet. But Becky and Zeyde . . . For hours, she'd sit on his lap, and the roars that came out of those two. . . . I'd be in the kitchen with Mama, helping her cook, and they'd be in the living room, he'd be tickling her feet, or she'd be teasing him. She used to imitate the way he scrunched up his face to shave – she got it perfectly, the way he pushed his nose aside – and you could hear her shrieks and his big belly laughs. Mama used to say, 'They'll bust a gut.' That's what she always said. 'They'll bust a gut.'"

She sighed. "But she had a temper, too, your mama did, Joey. Oh, boy, did she ever. That's why she and Zeyde fought so much – they were too much alike."

Again, Joey was incredulous. "Mama – and Zeyde – alike?"

Aunt Frieda nodded. "Like two peas in a pod. Hotheads."

Now there was sadness in her voice, and Joey was almost afraid to ask. "What happened?"

A long silence. "Everything was fine until our mama died. I was seventeen, Becky only fourteen. After that . . . things just went wrong. Becky got wilder and wilder . . . and she kept getting in trouble . . . and Zeyde got more and more upset."

"And then?"

There was an awkward pause. "And then she met your daddy and – and moved away."

"And what?" Joey said. "*What?*"

"And then you were born," Aunt Frieda said lightly, ruffling his hair.

"No! I mean when she moved away."

"I don't know, Joey. We lost touch."

"But –"

"That's enough now, Joey. You're here now – that's what matters."

Tell me! Joey wanted to shout, practically wriggling with frustration. He knew there was something Aunt Frieda wasn't saying, and he longed to know.

But she looked so sad, he didn't want to make her feel bad. And the way her mouth was set, closed tight, he didn't think he'd get any more out of her anyway.

Reluctantly, he let it go.

They had walked the entire block, past Cohen's Bakery, Stein's Hardware, and Kaplan's Produce, and had reached the corner. Aunt Frieda turned right.

"Where are we going, Mama?" Bobbie asked.

"Oh, I just want to stop at Yanofsky's and get Zeyde some of those kosher pickles he loves."

Yanofsky's.

Joey's heart started pounding. He didn't want to set foot in there.

"Uh . . . Mama . . . couldn't you go another time?" Bobbie asked.

"We're right here, Bobbie. It'll only take a minute."

Joey followed her inside. *I'll hold my tongue*, he vowed, *no matter what Mrs. Yanofsky says. I won't shame Aunt Frieda. Not after all she's done for me.*

But it was hard, because the minute they entered the store, the gossip started.

"Don't look now, but Frieda Rosen just came in with her *schvartze* nephew. . . ." Mrs. Yanofsky's shrill voice carried across the store.

People glanced at Joey. His cheeks flamed.

"That little brat . . . did you hear how he spoke to me last time he was in here?"

Heads shook disapprovingly. Joey wished Aunt Frieda would hurry so they could leave.

"A disgrace, that's what he is."

Several people gave Joey dirty looks.

"Undisciplined, just like his mother . . ."

Shut up, you witch! Joey thought, but he held his tongue. He glanced at Aunt Frieda. Chatting with the man at the deli counter, she appeared not to have heard. She got in line at the cash register, and Joey and Bobbie joined her. She smiled at them. "See, it only took a minute, and Zeyde loves these so."

". . . what do you expect from a mixed marriage? Of course, nothing good . . ."

Aunt Frieda's head jerked up.

The customer at the front paid and left. The line moved up. Now there was only one person between them and Mrs. Yanofsky.

"How they have the nerve to parade him around . . ."

Pink bloomed on Aunt Frieda's cheeks.

". . . with his *schvartze* blood. . . ."

The pink spread to Aunt Frieda's ears.

"A boy like that, bringing shame on the family . . ."

For a moment, Aunt Frieda seemed frozen. Then she thrust forward, pushing aside the woman in front of them, pushing aside Mrs. Yanofsky's hand that was out-stretched to take the customer's money. Aunt Frieda was shaking. But her voice, when she spoke, was low and measured. "*That boy*, Mrs. Yanofsky, is my nephew. My sister's son. My flesh and blood."

Mrs. Yanofsky's mouth fell open. Aunt Frieda put her arm around Joey's shoulder and hugged him to her. His heart thumped.

"There is nothing shameful about him." Aunt Frieda's voice rose. "Nor about my sister." She tossed the bag of pickles onto the counter and pulled Bobbie to her other side. "Nor about my family."

Mrs. Yanofsky backed up a step.

"And, Mrs. Yanofsky –" Aunt Frieda leaned forward, "if you ever expect to see me or any member of my family in this store again, you will stop telling lies about us – and mind your own business for a change!"

Aunt Frieda swept Joey and Bobbie out of the store. They stopped on the sidewalk. Aunt Frieda put one hand over her mouth and the other over her heart. Her eyes were large and startled-looking.

"Oh, my," she said in a strange voice.

"Mama, you were wonderful!" Bobbie said.

"I can't believe I just did that."

"You were grand!"

"Oh, my goodness."

"You told her, the old *yenta*."

"Bobbie!" Aunt Frieda protested. But her lips were twitching.

"Well, that's what you always call her," Bobbie said.

"I suppose I do."

All this time Joey had been unable to speak. Finally, he said, "Aunt Frieda?"

"Yes, Joey?"

"Will you be in trouble with Zeyde, too?"

Aunt Frieda laughed shakily. "Maybe." Then she patted his head. "No, of course not, Joey. I did what was right. Zeyde will understand."

I hope so, Joey thought.

Aunt Frieda shook her head. "Boy, that felt good!" She took each of them by the hand. "Come on, let's go home."

Joey skipped down Utica Avenue, one hand full of parcels, the other entwined with Aunt Frieda's.

My flesh and blood. My family.

Home.

18

After supper a few nights later, Zeyde took from the cupboard a glass that Joey had never seen before. It was the size of a regular small drinking glass, but it had Hebrew writing on it and – strangest of all – a candle inside, a short stubby candle that nearly filled it up. Joey wanted to ask what it was, but remembering how he'd got in trouble for not knowing about Shabbas, decided to keep quiet.

Aunt Frieda and Bobbie gathered around. Joey joined them. Zeyde lit a match, and reciting words that were different from the Shabbas prayers, lit the candle. He put the glass with the lit candle on the counter and then silently went out of the room, followed by Aunt Frieda.

"What's that?" Joey said to Bobbie.

"It's a *Yarzheit* candle. You light it on the anniversary of when someone died. It's to remember them."

"Who's this one for?"

"Bubbeh. Our grandma."

Joey remembered the first day he'd come to the house, when Zeyde had said, "She died almost thirteen years ago." Thirteen years – that was a long time to be without someone you loved. It had only been months since Mama died – and oh, how he missed her. He wished he could light one of those candles for her.

That night, Aunt Frieda and Bobbie went out to visit a friend of Bobbie's whose mother had just had a baby, Bobbie protesting all the way out the door that she didn't want to wear a dress. Joey looked at his Jackie Robinson clippings for a while, then found himself thinking about that candle in the kitchen and wondering what Zeyde was doing. He went downstairs. His grandfather was sitting in his usual chair by the window. On his lap was a photo album. Zeyde was taking a long time over each page, sometimes pulling the book closer to his face, sometimes running his fingers gently over a picture.

He must be looking at pictures of Bubbeh, Joey thought, and felt a swift pang of sorrow for his grandfather.

I wish there was something I could do. Joey wanted to go to Zeyde, comfort him somehow. But what would he say?

Joey remembered the picture of Bubbeh on Zeyde's bookcase. He could bring Zeyde the picture. "Here, Zeyde," he'd say, "this'll make you feel better."

But what if it didn't? What if Zeyde got mad at Joey for touching his things? *Besides*, Joey thought, *Zeyde probably wouldn't want to be comforted by me.*

Silently, he slipped away.

The newspaper lay open on the kitchen table. "Dodgers Posting Best Season in Six Years," screamed the headline, and, in smaller type: "On Track to Win NL Pennant."

In spite of himself, Joey sat down and started reading.

New York Daily News, August 20, 1947
Everything appears to be in place for the Brooklyn Dodgers to give their fans a present they've waited six long years for: the National League pennant. Sparked by the outstanding play of rookie sensation Jackie Robinson, the team has put together a winning streak that Brooklyn fans haven't seen since their last real pennant run, back in 1941, when "Leo the Lip" was at the helm. If the Dodgers keep playing like they have recently, they'll sew up the pennant within a week.

Sew up the pennant! Wouldn't that be something! Joey thought. Not that he cared one way or another, of course. But still, wouldn't it be swell, his first year in Brooklyn? Almost as if he'd brought them luck!

He thought about how Brooklyn would go nuts. They'd declare a holiday.

Quickly, he clipped the article and ran upstairs. As he was shoving it into his pillowcase, the other articles fell out, spilling onto the floor. Joey scanned the headlines.

At first they were all about Robinson. But slowly, unmistakably, they had begun to change. "Dodgers Are Giant-Killers." "Rally Gives Long-Suffering Brooklyn Fans Hope." "Boys in Blue are 'Dem Bums' No More."

Staring at the clippings, Joey had to admit it: he'd crossed the line. He was no longer just collecting Jackie Robinson stuff. Now he was collecting Dodgers stuff.

He didn't want to think about what *that* meant. Quickly, he gathered up the articles and stuffed them back into the pillowcase.

Several days later, a shriek brought Joey running downstairs. Bobbie jumped on him, thrusting the newspaper in his face.

"We did it! We did it! Look!"

Joey scanned the headline. "Dodgers Clinch NL Pennant!" Before he could stop it, he was smiling. "Wo —" He stopped short.

"Ha!"

Joey tried to look innocent. "What?"

"*Wha-at?*" Bobbie mimicked, smiling smugly. She pointed at him. "You've become a Dodgers' fan."

Joey busied himself searching for bagels and cream cheese in the refrigerator. "You're cracked."

"All right, mister, then why were you grinning like a baboon?"

Joey concentrated on spreading cream cheese on his bagel. "Because . . . the Yankees clinched four days ago, that's why."

"Didn't see you grinning then."

"And . . . I can't wait to see the Yanks whip the Dodgers in the World Series. Four straight."

"In your dreams."

"In your nightmares."

"Sure, sure. Big fan. Been clipping lots of Yankees articles lately?"

Did she know? She couldn't. He was sure he'd been too sneaky. He nodded. "My bulletin board's full of 'em."

"Mmm-hmm," Bobbie said smoothly. "Too bad you're such a rotten actor." She pointed at him. "Admit it, the Dodgers have finally won you over."

"No way!"

Bobbie just laughed.

Joey licked cream cheese from his fingers. He didn't so much as glance at the newspaper lying open on the table, nor did he say a word when Bobbie folded it up and put it in the garbage under the sink.

But later that evening, he spirited the sports section out of the pail, brushing away potato peels and onion skins – good thing Aunt Frieda hadn't dumped coffee grounds on it – and clipped out the article. In the privacy of his room, he devoured it.

"Dodgers defeat Cubs to win pennant by five games. . . . Robinson posts a homer and a steal in clinching game. . . . Big parade tomorrow through downtown Brooklyn. . . . Manager Burt Shotten predicts Series win over Yankees. . . ."

It was those last words that brought Joey up short. Because as he read them, he realized that Bobbie was right. *He had become a Dodgers fan.* He wanted the Brooklyn Dodgers to win the World Series. And not just win the Series – but win it against the New York Yankees!

For a moment, his conscience pricked him. How could he turn his back on the team he'd idolized since he was a little kid?

Like a cold you don't even realize you're catching until you start sneezing, the Dodgers had infected him. What with the way the fans had embraced Jackie Robinson, and the team had pulled together and figured out how to win, and what with gentlemanly Red Barber and the raucous Dodger Sym-*phony* Band, and the way the fans stayed loyal, year after losing year – well, he just couldn't help getting caught up in it. Dem Bums had won him over. And now he couldn't wait to cheer on the boys in blue, along with the rest of Brooklyn.

He pictured Bobbie's reaction: "I knew it! I told you so." No way! So now what?

Keep the collection hidden.

He started putting the clippings back into the pillow-case, but then stopped. There was a good chance that Bobbie was on to him – that girl's eyes were entirely too sharp. He had to find another hiding place. A better one.

But where? His eyes roved the room, alighting on the dresser, the bed, the closet. . . . The closet. The suitcase. That battered old suitcase he'd brought with him from Mrs. Webster's. Perfect!

He took the suitcase out of the closet, remembering the day he came – how long ago that seemed! – and hid the clippings inside. Then, as he was closing the suitcase, his hand felt something in a zippered compartment inside the top lid. He felt with his palm. It was flat and hard, like a large, thin book. Funny, he hadn't noticed it when he was unpacking.

He unzipped the compartment and reached inside. It wasn't a book because it had crimped metal edges. He gripped the thing and pulled it out.

Mama!

It was that picture! The one that used to sit on Mama's dresser. The one he'd wished he had.

Oh, how pretty she was! She was wearing a dress, and even though the picture was black-and-white, Joey remembered the red of that dress, cherry-red, with white diamond-shaped buttons and a sweeping white collar and a full skirt. She had on matching red shoes with curvy heels and a little hole in the front where her toes peeked out. She'd been wearing a hat – he remembered the hat, too, red felt with a sprig of white berries on the brim – but she'd taken it off. It was in her hand, hanging down at her side, and the other arm was stretched out, resting on a railing. Her hair was loose and full and curly. It must have been a windy day because her hair was blowing every which way, out from the sides, up in the back, and her head was slightly turned, as if she were trying to keep it out of her face. She was laughing and her whole face was smiling. Looking at her, Joey could hear that laugh, the deep chuckling sound that came from way down in her belly. She laughed as if nothing else could be as funny or as wonderful at that moment.

Joey clasped the picture to his chest. A lump filled his throat. One tear trickled, another, another, and then, for the first time since he'd wept in Mrs. Webster's arms, he gave way to grief. Rocking back and forth on his knees, holding the picture, holding himself, he howled.

When he finally subsided, wiping his eyes on his sleeve, he thought how strange it was that he hadn't known that Mrs. Webster had packed the photo in the suitcase. But thank goodness she had! It was so good to see Mama's face again. . . .

A thought struck. Maybe . . . Zeyde would love this picture. Though Zeyde hardly ever talked about Mama, and then only to say bad things, he must miss her terribly, just like Joey did. Maybe this picture would comfort Zeyde, the way the pictures in the photo album had comforted him the other night.

Joey knew that it was no accident that there were no pictures of Mama in the house; he knew that Zeyde had removed them all. But that was a long time ago. Maybe now he wished he had one. And this picture was so pretty, so *Mama*, how could Zeyde not love it?

And maybe . . . Zeyde would be so pleased at this gift, so impressed that Joey was giving him this precious thing, that he'd change his mind about Joey. Maybe he would *want* him to stay.

But even as he thought it, Joey knew that that wasn't why he wanted to give the picture to Zeyde. He wanted to give it to him . . . because . . . he loved him! The realization filled him with astonishment. And, Joey realized with a pang that brought fresh tears to his eyes, he wanted Zeyde to love him, too. Oh, if only Zeyde did! If only

Zeyde would hold him and hug him and be proud of him.

Through moist eyes, Joey looked at the picture again and felt a tug. This was his only picture of Mama, and he'd gone without it for so long. How could he part with it?

But he had to. He wanted to.

Cradling the photograph in his arms, Joey went downstairs.

Bobbie and Aunt Frieda were in the kitchen. He heard their low voices, the opening and shutting of cupboard doors as they put the supper dishes away.

He looked in the living room. Zeyde was in his chair by the window, just sitting, looking out at the street. The radio was silent, the room unlit, except for the soft glow of evening light.

"I . . . Zeyde . . ." Joey swallowed. "I have something . . ." He held out the picture. "Look, Zeyde. This is for you."

Zeyde looked. He went perfectly still. His face turned white. A spasm passed over it. Sudden tears filled his eyes. But then Zeyde rose, color flooding into his face, turning it crimson. He pointed his finger. "Get her out of my sight! Get out!" He swept the picture from Joey's grasp. It struck the arm of the chair and fell, glass shattering on the floor.

Joey stood frozen. Speechless. Then fury surged through him, and he found his voice. "I hate you!" he shouted. He ran from the room and bolted upstairs.

Joey tore into his room. He knew what was coming, and he wasn't waiting for Zeyde to send him away. Without even seeing what he was grabbing, he opened a dresser drawer and threw an armful of clothes into the still-open suitcase, then slammed it shut. Grabbed some coins, pushed the suitcase out the window, squeezed out after it, and climbed down the bars at the back of the house. Then he fled, blindly, not knowing or caring where he was going, half-running, half-walking, dragging the suitcase, fury driving him on.

He meant it. He hated Zeyde, hated him with every bit of hate he had in him –

Joey stopped. Where could he go? The image of a foster home, full of uncaring strangers, hit him. An orphanage, with other unwanted children . . . No!

Mrs. Webster! Yes, she'd take him in. In spite of all her bluster, she cared, he knew she did.

Running, dragging the suitcase, he caught a streetcar, transferred to the subway. Good thing he still knew how to get around. Uptown . . . uptown . . . He thought of Zeyde's face, contorted in anger . . . Aunt Frieda's hugs . . .

No. Don't think.

The suitcase bumped against his knees as he made his way from the subway station to his old apartment, vaguely aware of the familiar streets, the dark faces, the blare of blues from a car radio, the smell of an over-flowing garbage can. Up the stairs, lugging the suitcase . . .

He pounded on Mrs. Webster's door. No answer. Pounded harder. "Mrs. Webster! Open up, it's –"

The door across the hall opened – his old apartment! – and a man, wearing a sleeveless undershirt and boxer shorts, looked out. "What you doing, boy? What you banging down the house for?"

"Where's Mrs. Webster?"

The man shook his head. "Gone. Had one of those spells of hers, a bad one, and went into a nursing home."

Gone?

The man took a step closer. "You kin of hers?"

Joey looked up. "Huh? . . . No."

Before the man could say anything else, Joey bolted down the stairs.

Mrs. Webster gone. That meant . . . He trudged the few blocks to Miss MacNeill's office, trying to shut out any feelings at all, just putting one foot in front of the other. It was nighttime, so Miss MacNeill wouldn't be there, but he'd find a place to sleep, see her in the morning. . . .

He arrived at the building and crumpled onto the step, the suitcase on his knees.

Then it hit him. It was over . . . really over. Bobbie and Aunt Frieda, the neighborhood and the fellas, his room, his home – all smashed with the swipe of Zeyde's hand.

He'd thought he was changing Zeyde's mind, but he should have known better. It didn't matter how good he tried to be or how many prayers he memorized. Zeyde was never going to accept him.

Joey curled over the suitcase and sobbed, shoulders shaking, tears wetting his arms.

"Joey! Oh, my God!"

Joey jerked his head up.

Zeyde! Zeyde was running, stumbling toward him.

"Joey, thank God you're safe!"

Zeyde threw himself onto the step beside Joey, wrapped his arms around him and burst into tears. "Oh, Joey . . . I'm so sorry. . . ."

He was sorry! He was holding Joey, clinging for dear life, and it felt so good, Zeyde's strong arms holding him.

"Joey, I didn't mean it. . . ." Zeyde's chest heaved. "She left me, my Beckele . . . and then you –"

Broken cries.

"I drove her away . . . my temper, my stupid pride . . . all those years, filled with regret. . . . And then you – your face. . . . her face . . . It was her, all over again."

Zeyde buried his face in Joey's hair. "From the first moment you came . . . I was so scared . . ."

"Scared?"

Joey saw the fear in his dark eyes, shadowed under the cold streetlight. "Scared to make the same mistake – and then I did. . . . like a fool I did! Oh, Joey, I only wanted to keep you safe . . . but I didn't know how –"

Zeyde held him at arm's length. He gazed into Joey's face. "Joey . . ." A long, shuddering sigh. ". . . forgive me." His eyes were shiny and soft with tears. "Please, please . . . come home."

Joey looked Zeyde in the eye, gathering his courage. "Then . . . you won't ever send me away?"

"Joey, no! I would never – I could never let you go!"

Zeyde pulled Joey to him. Clinging to his grandfather, Joey's last sobs poured out. Finally, he wiped his eyes. He put his hand in Zeyde's.

"Yes, Zeyde . . . I'll come home."

19

Over the next several days, Joey and Zeyde spent hours talking about Mama. They told each other stories, sad ones and happy ones, and they cried and laughed and cried some more. They pored over photo albums. They walked around the neighborhood and visited Mama's favorite places: the streets where she rode her bike, the apple tree she climbed to steal the apples, the back stoop where she put on shows for the neighborhood kids.

One day when they were sitting together, Zeyde turned to Joey. "Joey," he said hesitantly, "did you ever hear of *shiva*?"

Joey shook his head.

Zeyde paused. "It's the way that Jews mourn for the dead. And . . . I have to tell you this. After I sent your mama away, to my everlasting regret, I sat *shiva* for her."

"But she wasn't dead!"

"I know, but . . . I was so angry it was as if she was dead to me." Zeyde's eyes filled with tears. "I'm sorry. I shouldn't have."

Joey's throat choked up. It wasn't fair of Zeyde. But as he swallowed down the tears, he saw that Zeyde truly was sorry.

An idea struck. "Zeyde," he said, "could we light one of those candles for Mama?"

"What candles?"

"Like the one you lit for Bubbeh. That would sort of bring Mama back to this house."

"In some ways you've already brought her home to me." Zeyde hugged him. "But yes, that's a wonderful idea. It hasn't been a year yet, but who cares? I'll teach you the prayer and we'll say it together. All right?"

"All right."

Several days later, Zeyde announced that he was going out to do an important errand. He came home with a parcel wrapped in brown paper under his arm, a smile tugging at his lips. He beckoned, and Joey followed him into the living room.

Zeyde unwrapped the parcel. *Mama!* It was the picture of Mama, newly framed with a fresh sheet of glass.

Zeyde placed it on the mantel with all the other

pictures. Together they looked at her; at the wild hair and the shining eyes and the laughing face.

"Isn't she beautiful?" Joey whispered.

Zeyde squeezed his hand. "She's home. Where she belongs."

The next day was Saturday. Somewhere between sleep and wakefulness, Joey felt someone nudging his shoulder. He opened his eyes to find Zeyde sitting on the edge of the bed.

"Joey, would you come to *schul* with me today?"

Joey bolted upright. "Really?" Then panic set in. "But . . . I don't know anything, Zeyde. The prayers . . . what to do . . ." *And I couldn't bear to make you ashamed of me.*

Zeyde smiled. "That's all right, you'll learn. Please, Joey. I would be proud to have you come with me."

Joey's heart filled. "Okay, Zeyde."

Soon they set out, Joey dressed in some of his new school clothes and carrying the velvet bag and the prayer book. Along the way, other grandfathers and grandsons joined them. Zeyde greeted each pair with a handshake and a smile. Then, his hand on Joey's shoulder, he said, "This is my grandson, Joey. Becky's boy. Isn't he the image of her?"

20

J oey clung to Zeyde's hand as they inched toward the turnstile. They were surrounded by Dodgers fans waiting to get into Ebbets Field. People jostled at the gold-rimmed ticket windows, hoping for last-minute seats. Teenage boys in sharp blue-and-white uniforms waved booklets in the air, hollering, "Program! Get ya program heah!"

"I can't believe I'm at the first game of the World Series." Bobbie looked as if she were afraid to blink in case it turned out to be a dream.

Joey felt the same way, but he didn't say so. Instead he squirmed miserably. In his back pocket was his Yankees cap. But he couldn't wear it. It would be a lie — he just didn't care about the Yankees anymore. Yet he couldn't root for the Dodgers either, not in front of Bobbie and

Zeyde. Here he was in Ebbets Field, longing to cheer and throw his arms in the air – and he couldn't.

They passed the turnstile and made their way to their seats, high up, midway between third base and home plate. Trying not to show his eagerness, Joey looked around. The base paths formed a perfect diamond. The infield was raked so smooth that the toothmarks of the rake were still visible in the reddish-brown dirt. Beyond it stretched the outfield, its fresh-mowed grass a brilliant green. 1947 WORLD SERIES: GAME 1 said the scoreboard. Beside the scoreboard, a sign proclaimed: ABE STARK CLOTHING – Hit This Sign, Win a Suit!

Had anybody ever hit it? Joey wondered. *I bet Jackie Robinson could!*

Down below, the umpire swept clean a gleaming home plate. The organ played "Take Me Out to the Ball Game." Smells of popcorn and hot dogs mingled in the air. All around Joey was a sea of blue and white.

If only he could be wearing those colors, too!

Beside him, Bobbie and Zeyde were giggling about something. Then Bobbie whispered, "Go on, Zeyde."

Zeyde turned to Joey. He reached into his back pocket, pulled out a Dodgers cap and handed it to him. "Go on, put it on," he said.

"But . . . but I –"

"Oh, come off it," Bobbie said. "We know all about you. Mama found your collection of Dodgers articles in your pillowcase ages ago."

Joey's face grew warm. "She did?"

"Zeyde knew, too," Bobbie said smugly.

Zeyde smiled. "That day we listened to the game on the radio, the look on your face when Robinson got spiked . . . and then when the team rallied around him . . . it wasn't too hard to figure out."

Joey covered his face with his hands and groaned.

"We were just waiting for you to admit it," Bobbie said. "Only you wouldn't, you big lummox."

Zeyde held out the cap again.

With a sheepish smile, Joey snatched it and tugged it over his curls. "How do I look?"

Zeyde grinned. "Like a real Brooklynite."

Joey grinned back. Finally, he could show his true colors – blue-and-white! He took the cap off, waved it in circles over his head and put it back on. He jumped up and did a little dance in place. He raised his arms and yelled, "Wahoo! Go, Dodgers!"

Bobbie and Zeyde laughed. Joey laughed, too. Then he leaned back. "Whew! Now I can really enjoy the game."

Zeyde leaned close. "Especially since you came in the front way this time."

At the end of six innings, the score stood at four apiece. It stayed that way through two more innings.

In the bottom of the ninth, with the score still tied and the Dodgers at the plate, Jackie Robinson came into the on-deck circle. Awestruck, Joey watched as he warmed up with three bats at once, swinging them around in sharp, even bursts. He tossed away first one bat, then another, and stepped into the batter's box. The fans erupted with cries of "Show 'em, Robinson!" and "We love you, Jackie!"

The Yankee pitcher, Spec Shea, delivered a fastball. Robinson swung. With a sharp *crack*, the bat connected. The ball shot into left centerfield, and Robinson took off.

The fans rose to their feet, craning forward.

Safe at first!

Cheers echoed through the stadium.

PeeWee Reese came up next. He doubled, sending Robinson to third.

Now Dixie Walker came up to bat. Robinson took a few steps off third base. "Go on, Jackie!" yelled several fans, but Shea, throwing quickly to the third baseman, held him. Robinson waited for Shea to check the sign with Yogi Berra, the catcher, then took one step away . . . another. . . .

"Go on, Jackie!"

"Go for it!"

"You can do it, Robinson!"

Joey's heart pounded.

Shea checked third. Robinson danced forward and back, and a mighty holler went up from the crowd. Shea held onto the ball. Robinson moved out a step farther. Shea went into his windup. Reese started moving off second base. Robinson skipped out another step.

Then Shea released the ball, and it was a wild pitch. It landed in the dirt behind Berra. Robinson took off. Joey jumped to his feet, along with the rest of the crowd. A roar rose and echoed in the air above the stadium.

Berra dove for the ball. Arms pumping, head down, Robinson streaked for home. Gripping the ball, Berra lunged toward the plate. Robinson slid, face first, two black arms outstretched in front of him, sending up a spray of dirt.

The fans held their breath –

The umpire fanned his arms out to the sides.

"Safe!" yelled Joey, Bobbie, and Zeyde together. "He stole home!"

Three blue-and-white Brooklyn Dodgers caps flew up into the air.

Today in the United States and Canada, people of all colors and races live, go to school, and work together. But this wasn't the case in the 1940s. Those were days of open discrimination, when mixed marriages – and bi-racial children – were considered by many to be scandalous.

The separation of black from white was especially evident in sports. In the 1940s, professional baseball was all white. Talented African American athletes played in the American Negro Leagues. Many people believed that black players were every bit as good as white players, but segregation made that impossible to prove.

Until 1947. That was when Branch Rickey, the president of the Brooklyn Dodgers, decided it was time for a change. He set out to find a gifted black ballplayer to put on the team. He knew the individual he chose would need great athletic ability along with tremendous spirit and determination. He chose Jackie Robinson.

Robinson, the grandson of a slave, was born in Georgia and grew up in California. He excelled in four sports: baseball, football, basketball, and track. Branch

Rickey realized that many people would be outraged by Jackie's presence, and he warned his new rookie that he would face abuse. "Robinson," he said, "I'm looking for a ballplayer with guts enough not to fight back." Robinson promised he wouldn't.

The promise must have been hard to keep. From the first day Jackie Robinson stepped onto the field in a Brooklyn Dodgers uniform, he endured name-calling, objects thrown at him, physical assaults, hate mail, and death threats. Several teams threatened to strike rather than play against him. Some of his own teammates even signed a petition to have him removed from the team.

Jackie Robinson kept his head high and kept his word. He didn't fight back. He simply played his game.

Gradually, the Brooklyn fans embraced him – after all, the Dodgers were winning for a change! His teammates accepted him, even those who had initially opposed his presence. So did people across the country. By the end of the 1947 season, Jackie Robinson led his team in runs and hits, was tied for home runs, and led the league in stolen bases. He was named the National League Rookie of the Year. By 1949, he was the National League's MVP.

One more thing: "Stealing home" – that is, stealing home plate from third base – is one of the most difficult moves in baseball. Although Jackie Robinson didn't actually steal home in the first game of the 1947 World Series, he did steal home nineteen times during his career. He also stole the hearts and imaginations of countless fans, and in doing so, struck a powerful blow for civil rights.

ACKNOWLEDGMENTS

The author wishes to thank:

Ken Abramson

June Beynon

Sandra Diersch

Paul Galewitz

James and Lynn Hill

Jack Lesnik

Michael Lesnik

Alan Milstein

Duncan Rayside

Ruth and Bernie Rosenberg

Amy Schwartz

Bill Schwartz

Merri Schwartz

Mary Jack Wald